STRETCHIN' HEMP!

"I want you to get a good look," Brody said as he ripped the curtain down from the window. Outside, Wade could see carpenters working on the gallows.

"When it's finished," Brody continued, "I'm going to march you over there and put the rope around your neck — *personally*. And then I'm *personally* going to open the trap door under your feet. But there won't be any drop, Wade. You know why? Because I won't have any slack in the rope. Your neck won't break. You'll just strangle, real slow. Your face will turn black, and your tongue will swell up and stick out of your mouth. And I'll be there the whole time — laughing!"

Brody grabbed a handful of Wade's hair and shoved him forward, pressing his face against the glass window-pane.

"Look at it, Wade!" Brody shouted. "That's where you're goin' to die!"

JAKE FOSTER

THREE RODE SOUTH

PINNACLE BOOKS
WINDSOR PUBLISHING CORP.

PINNACLE BOOKS

are published by

Windsor Publishing Corp.
475 Park Avenue South
New York, NY 10016

First printing: May, 1990

Printed in the United States of America

Chapter 1

The three riders were trail worn and dusty. They sat on their weary horses at the crest of a long, gently rising hill. It had been a hard ride and a tedious one, that was for sure, but below them was their final destination, the end of the tiresome trail.

"Is that it?" asked the girl. She was dressed in men's clothing and wore a sixgun on her hip. Her hair was tucked up inside the wide-brimmed hat she wore, and like her two traveling companions, she needed a bath after the long days on the hot and dusty trail. But even the layers of trail dust caked on her by sweat and the men's riding clothes did not hide her natural beauty. She was young, probably not yet twenty.

"That's Drago," said the man to her right. "You sure you want to go through with this, Trish?"

"I'll see this through or die trying, Uncle Bob," said Trish. "If you and Pawnee want to back out, that's up to you. I've come too damn far now not to see it through."

"Who said anything about backing out?" said the third rider, the one called Pawnee. He sat astride a paint pony, leaning forward in the saddle, his arms resting across the saddle horn. He wore fringed buckskins, his trousers tucked into high-topped black boots. His buckskins, though stained and grimy, were beautifully decorated with colorful quillwork in floral designs. He carried a long knife in his belt and wore two Remington .44 revolvers at his hips, their handles facing forward. A Winchester .44 repeating rifle was sheathed in a scabbard that hung on the left side of his saddle.

"Trish," said the man she had addressed as Uncle Bob, "you got no call to talk to us like that. We come all this way with you, and we ain't crawfishing now. Bobby was your brother. I know how you felt about him and I ain't belittling that, but your father was my best friend and Bobby was my godson. He was named after me. Don't make light of my feelings on this matter either."

Trish looked at Robert D. Wade, the man she called Uncle Bob. He was not really her uncle. He was, as he had said, her father's best friend, and she had called him Uncle Bob all her life. He was a handsome man, hard and tough, and though he affected the rough language of the frontier, he was well educated and had been an officer in the Confederate Army during the war. Bobby had been away from home for some time when the border ruffians had come to the Madison home and killed their parents. Trish, only fifteen years old at the time, had hidden in the woods, terrified. It had been three long days before Uncle Bob had happened by to check on them. He had discovered the burned house and the frightened girl. He had buried her parents for her, and then he'd taken her in. He had taken care of her, had raised her, and had taught her many things . . . not the kinds of things most girls were taught. He had taught her to ride and rope and shoot. He had made her tough, like he was tough. She had stayed with him, and he had become like a father to her.

But they had never been able to find Bobby. They had looked, and they had heard about him, of course. They heard that Bobby had killed a man in El Paso and then another in Abilene. They had both been fair fights, but Bobby was beginning to acquire a reputation as a killer, as a man to be feared. Then there had been the shootout in Deadwood that everyone knew about, the shootout between Bobby and Kid Conley, in which Bobby had dropped the Kid with one shot to the head. Because of the

Kid's notoriety, that was the gunfight that had made Bobby's reputation almost overnight. It seemed as if everyone was talking about Bobby Madison. And then the dime novels had begun to appear. The first one Trish had ever seen had been called *Bobby Madison: Fighting Man of the Wild West*. The drawings in the book hadn't looked anything like the real Bobby, and the daring deeds described in the fanciful story had been outlandish, sometimes impossible. Other books followed: *Bobby Madison and the Gauchos of the Pampas, Bobby Madison and the Train Robbers, Bobby Madison the Frontier Scout, Bobby Madison's Daring Daylight Raid, The Bloody Trail of Bobby Madison*. Trish had bought them all and had read them with mixed feelings. She knew they were lies, and she knew that her brother's name was being used to make profits for unscrupulous writers and publishers. Yet she couldn't help but enjoy seeing her brother being built up as a romantic hero. Then the news story had appeared. Bobby had been killed in a town called Drago by a sheriff named Phil Brody, and one more dime novel had come after that. It had been called *The Death of Bobby Madison,* and it presented the world with a new hero: Sheriff Phil Brody.

At first Trish had wondered if Bobby had really gone bad, if he had become a bad outlaw. It had been years since she had seen him. How could she know? He had been so young when the war started, and he had left his home and the influence of his parents at a tender age. Such experiences had turned the heads of other young men. But other news reports came out, and she began to hear stories. Finally, Uncle Bob had met a man in a saloon in Waco. He had brought the man out to their camp to see Trish. The man had recently come from Drago and he knew Sheriff Phil Brody — knew him and did not like him. He claimed to have witnessed the killing, and he said that Brody had shot Bobby in the back. Bobby had not been wanted for anything but had he been famous, and Brody had wanted to capitalize on that reputation. He wanted to be known as the man who killed Bobby Madison. And that, the man had said, had been the whole truth.

All of this flashed through Trish's mind in a moment as she sat there in the saddle between Robert D. Wade and Pawnee O'Rourke, looking down into the town of Drago, the town in which her brother had been murdered by an ambitious and cowardly lawman.

"I didn't mean anything by it," she said. "Let's go down."

"Hold on, gal," said Robert D. "Remember what we talked about. Don't let on who you are or why we're here. Don't make any moves toward Brody. We get us a couple of rooms in the hotel, get cleaned up, eat a decent meal, and maybe have a drink or two. Then we get a good night's sleep. We take some time and learn what we can about the town and about Brody. Then we make our plans."

"I know, Uncle Bob," said Trish. "Don't worry about me. I can control myself."

She kicked her black stallion in the sides and started down the hill toward Drago, Robert D. Wade and Pawnee O'Rourke right behind her. On their way down the hill, the three riders saw the large house that sat just outside of town. Two stories high with a covered veranda running all the way around, the house was decorated with fine scroll-work around its shuttered windows and along its over-hanging eaves. It was painted in two shades of blue and appeared to be totally out of place there on the flat brown and yellow prairie just outside the small frontier town. It had a backyard enclosed by a white picket fence, and as they drew nearer, they saw a small crowd clustered at the gate. They slowed down to watch. There was a man just inside the gate who appeared to be allowing the people outside to come in one at a time.

"Reckon what's going on there?" asked O'Rourke.

Wade nudged his roan a little forward for a better look. Trish and Pawnee followed. In the center of the backyard behind the blue house was a granite spire, a pile of rocks at its base.

"A grave," said Trish. "It must be someone's funeral."

A chill gripped her, and Trish shuddered as she thought

8

about Bobby and wondered where his grave might be. She wondered if he had gotten a funeral and, if so, who had attended. Then she purposefully pushed the sad, grim thoughts out of her mind and replaced them with anger and hatred, both directed at the coward who had shot Bobby in the back for no reason other than to make himself famous—to make himself famous at Bobby's expense, at her expense, at the expense of everyone who knew her brother and loved him. She longed with bitterness to see Phil Brody, but she knew that she would have to control herself when that time came. She would have to hide her anger and her hatred, but when the right time came, Brody would know. Sheriff Phil Brody. He would know. He would not get it in the back the way he had given it to Bobby. He would be facing his killers, and he would know who they were and why they had come. He would know the reason for his untimely and violent death. Trish would see to that.

They rode on into the town, past a saloon and a billiard hall, and stopped in front of the Grand Hotel. At two stories high with an elaborate facade and a balcony over the board sidewalk, it was not much larger than the blue house, and it was not nearly as impressive. They tied their horses to the hitch rail in front and went inside. A young man behind the counter stood up to greet them as they approached.

"Howdy, folks," he said. "Can I help you?"

"We need two rooms," said Robert D. "Be nice if they was next door to each other. One for the lady, one for the two of us."

The clerk turned the register around and placed a lead pencil on top of it.

"If you'll just sign the book," he said, "I'll get your keys. How long you folks going to be staying with us? You here for the big celebration?"

"That's right," said Robert D. He had no idea what big celebration the man was talking about, but it sounded like a good reason to be stopping in town. "I don't know just how long we'll stay. Any problem with that?"

9

"Oh, no," said the clerk. "No, sir. It's lucky for you, though, that you got here early. Another two, three days, you won't be able to find a room anywhere in Drago. No, sir. Place will be packed."

"For the big celebration," said Pawnee.

"That's right," said the clerk. He had a big smile on his face.

"Where can we get a bath?" said Trish.

"Barber shop just down the street and on the other side," said the happy clerk. "Anything I can help you with, just let me know. My name's Purlie."

Purlie put three keys on the counter.

"I think that's all we need for now, Purlie," said Robert D., picking up the keys. He handed one to Pawnee and one to Trish, keeping the third one for himself. "Where's the rooms?"

"Just up the stairs," said Purlie. "First two rooms on the right."

The three travelers went back outside to get their saddle rolls, then they went upstairs to their rooms. Each unpacked a change of clothes. They went back downstairs and were on the way out the front door when Robert D. turned back toward the counter.

"Where's the livery stable?" he asked.

"Far end of the street," said Purlie. "This side."

They walked their horses down the street to the livery stable, where they paid a man named Brannon to feed, brush, and stable the animals. Then they walked back down the street to the barber shop.

"We need baths," said Robert D. The barber and the man in the chair getting his face shaved stared at the trio. "What's wrong?"

"Uh . . . nothing, mister," said the barber, looking at the guns on the hips of the three. "It's just that we don't usually get ladies coming in here."

"I'm no lady," said Trish, "but I still need a bath."

"I'll have my boy draw the water," said the barber.

After a short wait, Trish was in the back room, where a tub of hot water sat in the middle of the floor. There was a

10

back door to the room, but it was latched securely from the inside. She knew that Robert D. and Pawnee were out front in the barber shop, so feeling perfectly safe in spite of the lack of a latch on the front door, she stripped off her filthy trail clothes. Naked, she tested the water. It was hot, but not too hot. She stepped into the tub and allowed herself to sink down as far as she could. She would have liked to stay a while and luxuriate in the soothing bath, but she knew that Robert D. and Pawnee were waiting their turns. She also knew that they had urgent business, and there was much to find out before they could make their plans. She would hurry her bath and get out.

A tall, slender man — slender except for the pot belly that protruded in front and hung out over his belt buckle — stepped inside the barber shop from the sidewalk. He wore dark blue, almost black, trousers and shirt. His boots, into the tops of which his trousers were tucked, and his vest were black leather, and his hat was a black Plainsman with a red band. He wore two Colts, slung low, their holsters strapped to his thighs, and a yellow bandanna was tied around his neck. He looked to be a man about thirty years old. His face was smooth and clean, and a star was pinned to the left side of his vest.

"Howdy, Warren," said the barber, and he sounded friendly enough, but Robert D. thought that he could detect a little uneasiness in the barber's voice.

The man gave the barber a slow nod and stared at the two strangers who stood, one on either side of the door to the back room, leaning on the back wall. He walked casually across the room and reached a long arm out toward the door handle.

"I wouldn't," said Robert D.

Pawnee's hands were twisted inward and resting on the butts of his Remingtons. Robert D. was standing calmly, his arms folded across his chest. The dark-suited man hesitated, his hand still gripping the door handle. His eyes were fixed on those of Robert D. Finally, the barber broke the silent tension in the room.

"There's a lady back there, Warren," he said. "Taking a

11

bath."

The man called Warren smiled a sideways smile and snorted. He looked over his shoulder at the barber, then back at Robert D.

"Hell, I won't bother her none," he said, and he started to push the door. Robert D. put a firm hand against the man's chest and held him back. At the same time, the man felt the barrel of one of Pawnee's Remingtons touch the base of his skull, and he heard the unmistakable click of the hammer being thumbed back. He hadn't pushed the door open more than two inches, and he slowly pulled it shut again. Still staring into Robert D.'s eyes, he gave another snort, turned and walked back across the room, and went outside again. The sound of the barber's stored-up breath being released was audible to all in the room. Pawnee eased the hammer of his Remington back down and replaced the revolver in its holster.

"Gents," said the barber, "you'd better watch your step in this town from now on."

"Who is he?" said Robert D.

"That's Warren Sneed, one of Phil Brody's deputies. You've heard of Brody?"

"Seems like I've heard that name," said Robert D.

"He's the man who killed Bobby Madison," said the barber. "Hell, man, he's famous. There's a book about him."

"Already?" said Robert D.

"Well, it was done local. Newspaper editor here wrote it and printed it up. You can buy a copy most anywhere in town. Anyhow, Sheriff Brody and his deputies got ahold of this town by the short hairs. Like I said, you better watch your step. All three of you."

"Les," said the man in the chair, his face still half covered with lather, "you going to finish this job?"

"Keep your britches on," said Les. "I'll have your face just as smooth as a baby's butt in just another couple of minutes."

"Hold out your hand first," said the man. "I want to see if you quit shaking. I don't want my throat cut."

"Aw, shut up," said Les.

The door to the back room came open, and Trish stepped out into the front room. She was still dressed like a man, but her clothes were clean and fresh, and her hair was wet. She had her hat in one hand and the bundle of her old trail clothes in the other. They were wet. Obviously, she had washed them in the tub following her bath. Her Colt .36 hung at her right side. Both Les the barber and his customer stared at her for a moment. They couldn't help themselves. She was a rare sight, a beautiful young woman dressed like a man and toting a six-shooter. Then, recalling the protectiveness of the two hardcases by the back door, they forced themselves to look away.

"Well, get on with it," said the impatient customer.

Les grabbed the man's nose by the nostrils, cutting off his breath and forcing his mouth to open, and began to scrape with the razor above his customer's upper lip.

"That feels a whole lot better," said Trish. "Which one of you two is next?"

When all three had bathed, changed, and stashed their trail clothes back in the hotel rooms, they went outside again. Robert D. pointed with his chin to a place across the street.

"Let's try that," he said.

Looking across the street, Trish read the sign.

"Maude's Fine Food?" she asked.

"Yeah."

They walked across the street, avoiding men riding horseback and driving wagons. The traffic was coming from all directions, and it was heavy. The big celebration, whatever it might be, was apparently already drawing the people to Drago.

As they opened the door to Maude's Fine Food and went inside, Warren Sneed watched. He was lounging against the wall a few doors down the street. Beside him was another man whose clothing was almost identical to Sneed's. Sneed nodded his head in the direction of

13

Maude's.

"That's them," he said. "Real hardasses."

His partner, shorter and chunkier than Sneed, licked dry lips. His eyes were narrow slits.

"That's a hell of a looking female they got with them," he said. "Bet she's a wild one."

Chapter 2

Maude's food was fine, they decided. Maude cooked, and her husband Claude waited tables and collected the money. Claude was a gregarious fellow, and since Robert D. and his companions had wandered into the place at an odd hour and were, therefore, the only customers, Robert D. decided to take advantage of Claude's nature.

"What's this big celebration we been hearing about?" he asked.

"Oh," said Claude, "it's the town's twenty-fifth birthday. It's going to be a dandy. Lots of food and beer. Fiddling contests. Fireworks. A band for dancing in the street. Speechmaking. Parade. You all come to town for that?"

"Well," said Robert D. between bites of his steak, "we was just traveling through. Heading west. A man we met on the road told us there was a big celebration coming up down here, so we decided to take it in. We figured we could use a rest from the trail anyhow. So it seemed like a good excuse."

Trish and Pawnee listened carefully. They had actually, of course, ridden south to Drago on purpose. Robert D. was fabricating stories for the Drago residents in order to hide their intentions, and they wanted to make sure that anything they might say later on would match with his lies.

"Well, y'all picked a good time to happen by," said Claude. "It's going to be a good one. They're even saying that folks'll come in from the capitol for it. Phil Brody—

15

that's our sheriff, Phil Brody, you might've heard of him — Phil Brody's got big ambitions . . . political ambitions, you might say. He wants to be governor. At least that's what everyone's saying. He's the one that planned all this."

"It seems like I have heard of Brody," said Robert D. "Phil Brody. Wasn't he in the news lately? Killed some gunfighter, didn't he?"

"Yeah," said Claude. "Bobby Madison. There's a book about it. I got copies for sale right here. Right over there on the counter by the register. Fifty cents. Just about every store in town has them for sale."

Pawnee took the last bite of his meal and gulped down what was left of his coffee. The others were only about half finished with theirs. He wiped his mouth on his sleeve and stood up from his chair. Walking over to the counter, he found the stack of books and picked one up. Then he went back to his spot at the table and sat down with it. Claude got up and went for the coffeepot. He refilled everyone's cup, took the pot back, then resumed his seat with his only customers. Pawnee was leafing through the book. Trish was aching to ask some direct questions and to rip the book from Pawnee's hands, but she managed to restrain herself. Robert D. was right. He knew what he was doing.

"It says here," said Pawnee, "that Brody brought peace to Drago by wiping out the Bobby Madison Gang. Madison, it says, was the only one left when he and Brody faced each other down out on Main Street."

"Is that right?" asked Robert D. "Did he get the others right here in town, too?"

"Actually," said Claude, "I never even knew there was a gang until that book come out. I guess he got them somewhere out of town. I don't know. Really, all I know about it is just what it says in that book."

"Did you see the shoot-out?" asked Trish.

"Where did it happen?" asked Pawnee, standing and walking over to the window. "Right out there?"

"I . . . uh . . . I didn't see that, either," said Claude.

"Well, you must have heard somebody who did. Everybody in town must have been talking about it," said Robert

16

D.

"You know," said Claude, suddenly lowering his voice and speaking confidentially to the trio, "I don't know anyone who actually seen it happen. You know, actually seen it. One day the word started spreading that Brody had killed Bobby Madison sometime the day before. Then later that book come out. Just between you and me — Well, never mind."

Trish took a sip of coffee and swallowed hard.

"Is . . . uh . . . is this . . . Madison . . . buried around here?" she asked.

"Oh, yeah," said Claude. "Sure. That's going to be one of our main attractions. Big tourist attraction. Which way did you all come into town?"

"From the north," said Robert D.

"Then you seen it. You had to. Big monument. It's right in Phil Brody's backyard."

"The big blue house?" asked Trish.

"That's it. The grave's right in the backyard. Has a big granite marker."

"Well, we saw people gathered up at the gate there," said Trish. "The funeral couldn't have been going on just today."

"No, no," said Claude. "That wasn't no funeral you seen. Brody charges a dime for folks to go into the yard and see the grave. It's got Bobby Madison's picture on it and everything. For fifty cents you can take one of the stones off the pile for a souvenir . . . a keepsake, if you're so inclined. That's what the guards are there for."

Trish clinched her teeth until her jaws hurt. Robert D. saw, and he slipped a hand under the table and gripped her knee hard.

"Drago must pay its sheriff awful good," said Pawnee. "I never knowed a sheriff before with a house like that one."

"Well, he . . . uh . . . he's not just the sheriff," said Claude. "He's kind of the mayor, too, I guess. Something like that."

"The town council must have a high opinion of the man," said Robert D. "You got some more of that coffee?"

Claude went after the pot again. As he returned to the

17

table with it, he answered Robert D.

"We got no council. Brody sort of has that responsibility, too. I guess. That authority . . . whatever. The fact is, Brody's just about all the government we got here in Drago. He's it. Him and his deputies. His army, you might say. He collects taxes, and all us merchants pay him a fee for protection."

Robert D. stood up and stretched. Then he dug into his pocket for some change.

"Well," he said, "I better pay you for this food and that there book. Then I guess we'll wander on around the town for a bit. Take in the local tourist attractions."

They stood for a while, some distance from the big blue house. A few people were in the yard, standing around the grave. Trish was taking deep breaths, trying to regain control of her anger and her hurt. Finally, the people left the yard, and there were two guards there alone. They were dressed the same way as Warren Sneed.

"Brody's army," said Robert D. "They've even got uniforms."

"Reckon how many of them they are?" asked Pawnee.

"That's one of the things we have to find out. You all right, Trish? We don't have to do this. Not right now."

"I'm fine, Uncle Bob," she said. "Let's go."

They walked on over to the gate, where they were met by one of the dark-suited guards.

"You come to see the grave?" he asked.

"Yeah," said Robert D.

"Be ten cents apiece," said the guard.

Robert D. gave the man three dimes, and the guard opened the gate to let them in. Trish could feel her heart pounding beneath her breast. Her emotions were strange and mixed. She had not seen Bobby for years, and now she was about to visit his grave. Part of her felt like she was going to her brother's funeral, but she had been charged an entry fee. It was like going to a sideshow. Resentment and indignation welled up from deep within her. And the worst of it all was that she had to repress all of those emotions.

She had to approach the granite spire like any other curious and unemotional sightseer. Robert D. knew what she was going through. He, himself, had similar emotions, and he, too, had to push those feelings somehow, somewhere into the back of his mind. But he had to restrain himself, too, in another way. He had to restrain the powerful, fatherly impulse to put an arm around Trish and hold her close, to comfort her and tell her that everything was going to be all right.

Pawnee was the least personally involved of the three, yet even he was not free of powerful feelings at this moment. These were the two best friends he had, had ever had, more than that. They were really the only friends he had ever had. He had not known Bobby Madison, had never seen the man, and if he had not known and loved Trish and Robert D., he would likely have believed the rumors and the dime novels about Bobby. So Pawnee's feelings were for the living, not for the dead.

They walked on over to the grave. A mound of fist-sized granite rocks had been formed over the grave itself, and at the head of the mound stood the granite spire. There was an inscription on the spire, but it said only: "Bobby Madison, Killed by Phil Brody." Brody's name was written larger than Bobby's. Beneath the inscription, a photograph was framed and set into the granite spire. It was a photograph of Bobby Madison's body. His arms had been folded across his chest and a six-gun placed in each of his hands. The body had been strapped to a board, and standing beside the upright board, holding it up with one hand and smiling, was a man in a black suit with a waxed handlebar mustache. His left hand brushed aside the lapel of his jacket to hook a thumb in his vest. Below the hand a badge was visible, pinned on the vest. There was a caption beneath the photograph that read: "Bobby Madison, the outlaw, in death, with Sheriff Phil Brody, his Killer."

Trish wanted to lash out at the guards who stood by watching her. She wanted to smash the ghastly photograph. She wanted to go on a roaring rampage, to kill and destroy, but she knew that she had to remain calm on the outside. She had to appear to be nothing more than a curiosity seeker, a tourist, and she suddenly developed a hatred for tourists and sightseers. She wanted to cry. She took a deep breath and walked around the grave. As she moved around to the backside of the spire so that she was facing the rear of the blue house, she noticed another large pile of the fist-sized granite rocks up against the back of the house.

"Well, we seen it," said Robert D. "You all ready to go?"

"You can take one of them rocks off the grave for a souvenir for fifty cents," said one of the guards. Robert D. and Trish looked into each other's faces, and Trish gave a nod. Robert D. reached into his pocket.

"Sure," he said. "Let us have one."

He gave the man fifty cents.

"Just help yourself," said the guard.

"Grab one, Pawnee, would you?" said Robert D., and he put an arm around Trish's shoulder, turning her with him to leave the yard. He knew that she couldn't take much more of this without losing control. Trish had always been blunt and direct, had always been one to state her mind no matter what. And he, himself, felt a rage building from deep within.

"Come on, honey," he said.

They had only walked a few steps away from the gate. Pawnee was right behind them. Robert D. could feel the tension in Trish's shoulders and back.

"Uncle Bob," she said, her voice trembling with barely controlled rage.

"Don't say a damn thing, Trish," said Robert D. "Not yet."

They walked without speaking again all the way back to the Grand Hotel. As they passed by the desk, Robert D. spoke over his shoulder without slowing down.

"Send up a bottle of good whiskey, Purlie," he said.

They walked on up the stairs, unlocked the door to the first room, and went inside. Trish sat stiffly on the edge of the bed.

"Damn them," she said.

"Not yet," said Robert D. "Hush."

There was strained silence in the room for another moment. Then they heard footsteps coming up the stairs. Purlie appeared at the door with a bottle and three glasses. Robert D. paid him, while Pawnee took the bottle and glasses and poured three drinks. As Purlie was going back down the stairs, Robert D. shut the door. Pawnee held a glass out toward Trish. She stared at it for a moment in silence.

"I don't want that," she said finally.

"Drink it," said Robert D.

Trish took the glass and drank the whiskey down. The sudden burning in her throat caused her to cough, but she recovered quickly and handed the empty glass back to Pawnee.

"Give me another one," she said.

"I know that was hard for you," said Robert D. "Maybe you shouldn't have gone."

"I had to, Uncle Bob. As awful as it was, I had to see it. Where is that damn Brody anyhow? I haven't seen him anywhere."

"It's just as well," said Robert D. "We'll see him soon enough."

Pawnee refilled his own glass and that of Robert D. Trish was still sipping at her second.

"Even selling the goddamn rocks," she said. "You see that pile of rocks by the house? Damn."

"Yeah," said Pawnee. "They sure don't intend to run out anytime soon, do they?"

Pawnee's heart ached for Trish. He longed to take her in his arms and comfort her, but he could not. She was like a daughter to Robert D., and the hugging and comforting was part of his role. Still, he ached for her.

"Where is that damn rock?" asked Trish.

Pawnee picked it up from the table where he had placed it upon entering the room. He held it in front of his chest.

"Here," he said.

"Let me have it."

He handed her the rock and Trish took it in her right hand, then drew back as if to fling it with all her strength into the wall. Robert D. caught her fist just before her forward motion began. He took the rock away from her and gave it back to Pawnee.

"Damn it, Trish," he said. "It's hard. But you've got to control yourself. No one can know who we are or why we're here or how we feel about Bobby or Brody or anything else. No one. Not yet. We don't know yet what we're up against here. We came here for two reasons. Three maybe. We wanted to find out what really happened to Bobby."

"We found out," she said. "He was murdered."

"We came to pay our respects to his remains. We found him and done that."

"And we came to kill Brody," said Trish.

"But we found out some other things," said Robert D. "Brody has got an army to protect him here in Drago. He runs this whole town like he's a king. It's not going to be easy to get him without getting ourselves killed. So we've got to go at this slow and easy. And we can't give ourselves away. As long as they don't know who we are or why we're here, we got an edge. We don't want to lose that edge."

"I know, Uncle Bob," said Trish. "I'll be all right. It was just . . . seeing it like that. Like it was part of a circus or something."

"Yeah," said Robert D., "and it could get worse. You might have to watch Brody playing the big shot, listen to him brag about what he done, what he done to Bobby. You might hear all kinds of lies told about Bobby. And you'll have to watch it all and listen to it like it don't matter to you one way or the other."

"For how long, Uncle Bob?" Trish asked.

"Until we know that we're ready."

"We got another job to do now," said Trish, "and it's going to make it even harder."

"What's that?"

"We've got to take Bobby home. We can't leave him here like that."

Chapter 3

They had a few more drinks, and Trish fell asleep. She was not a teetotaler, neither was she a heavy drinker. Robert D. pulled her boots off her feet.

"She'll be all right," he said. "Let's you and me go try out one of the local saloons."

They left Trish in the bed and locked the door, then went downstairs and outside. Looking up and down the street, they decided to try the Tanglefoot, directly across from the Grand Hotel. It seemed to be the largest and the most popular place on the street. The sun had not yet gone down, but it was low in the western sky. Soon it would be the busiest time of day for the Tanglefoot or any other such establishment. Walking into the saloon, the two strangers didn't get more than a cursory glance from any of the other customers. As Purlie had told them earlier in the hotel, the celebration would bring lots of people to town. The local residents were expecting to see strangers in droves. Robert D. and Pawnee paused for an instant just inside the swinging doors and looked the place over. It already had a good crowd. There were still places to be had at either the bar or at tables, but judging by the size of the early crowd, Robert D. figured it wouldn't be long before the place was packed. At a table against the wall to their far right-hand side, Robert D. saw Warren Sneed and two other uniformed deputies sitting together. They didn't seem to be doing anything but watching the crowd.

"Come on," said Robert D., and he led the way on over to the bar. The bartender saw the two new customers approaching, and he met them just as they leaned forward on their elbows on his bar.

"What'll it be, gents?" he said.

"Bourbon County whiskey," said Robert D.

"Same," said Pawnee.

The bartender put out two glasses and poured them full. Robert D. paid for the drinks.

"Them . . . uh . . . lawmen over there," he said. "They just guarding the place?"

"Well, yeah," said the bartender. "You might say that."

"Is that normal in this town?"

"It's normal here at the Tanglefoot. You see, Sheriff Brody owns this place. His men make sure that nobody makes any trouble in here."

"Oh," said Robert D. "Give us another shot, will you?"

The bartender refilled the glasses, and Robert D. paid him again.

"We just got into town today," he said. "Already heard a lot about this Brody. Even went down to see the local shrine, but I don't think we've seen anything of the local hero yet."

"Brody's out of town. Some kind of business at the capitol. He'll be back in time for the celebration, though. You can count on that. You'll see plenty of him then, if you're still in town."

"Oh, we'll be here," said Pawnee. "Wouldn't miss that for love nor money.

"Hey, Burl," someone shouted from the far end of the bar to Robert D.'s left, "how about some service down here."

"Don't wet your pants," shouted Burl the bartender. "I'm coming."

"Leave the bottle," said Robert D., tossing some coins on the bar.

Burl hustled off to take care of other customers, and just then Warren Sneed stepped up to the bar just to

Robert D.'s left. The deputy leaned on the bar with his left elbow so that he was facing Robert D., his right arm free. Robert D. glanced at Sneed, then looked back to the front. With his peripheral vision, he saw that another deputy had sidled up to Pawnee's right.

"We meet again," said Sneed.

"I don't recall meeting you at all," said Robert D. "There never was no formal introduction."

"I can take care of that," said Sneed. "I'm Warren Sneed, deputy sheriff. I work for Phil Brody. I'm sure you've heard of Brody."

"Not before I come into this town earlier today," said Robert D., lying. "But ever since I got here, I ain't heard much of anything else."

"He's a big man," said Sneed. "This is his town."

"Where I come from, a big man don't have to go around tooting his own horn all the time," said Robert D. "That monument out in his backyard is about the gaudiest thing I ever did see. Who's your friend?"

With that question, Robert D. gave a nod toward the deputy standing on Pawnee's right side.

"Oh," said Sneed, "that's Dexter Beeler, but it seems to me that I been making all the intros. What's your name, mister?"

"Is it important to you?"

"It's my business," said Sneed. "I keep track of all the strangers who come through Drago, especially hardcases."

"Robert D. Wade," said Robert D. "And this is Pawnee O'Rourke."

Sneed leaned forward on the bar in order to look across Robert D. and Pawnee at his companion, Beeler.

"Dex," he said, "you hear that? Do the names Robert D. Wade and Pawnee O'Rourke mean anything to you?"

"Seems like I've heard them someplace before," said Beeler. "Can't be sure."

"On some wanted poster, maybe, huh?" asked Sneed.

"Probably," said Beeler.

"Well," said Pawnee, deciding to inject himself into the discussion, "you boys go on back and rummage through

25

your dodgers. If you find us in there, be sure and let us know."

"You're wanted, ain't you?" asked Sneed.

"Not here, Sneed, so it's none of your business," said Robert D. "You can quit drooling."

"Yeah. Well, I'll check on that."

"Do."

Sneed turned from the bar and started to walk away, but he changed his mind. He stopped and spoke once more to Robert D. over his shoulder.

"Where's the little gal?" he asked.

"She's safe," said Robert D. "Don't worry."

"What's her name?"

"She's my niece," said Robert D., lying just a little. "We call her Trish."

"I'll give you a bit of advice, Wade. Don't go out at night. Watch your back. Better yet, get out of town. You never know what might happen."

He waved a limp wrist at Beeler, and the two uniformed deputies walked back across the crowded room to their table and resumed their seats. They continued to stare at Robert D. and Pawnee.

"That supposed to get us scared?" asked Pawnee.

"I guess. One thing we done wrong, Pawnee."

"What's that?"

"We didn't mean to call attention to ourselves just yet."

"Well, Robert D., we didn't really have much choice, now, did we?"

Robert D. reached for the bottle and poured two more drinks.

"I guess that's right," he said. "It's still unfortunate."

He picked up his glass and took a long sip. Pawnee picked up his and drained it.

"It's just them two so far," he said.

Robert D. turned his head and looked at Pawnee as his partner poured himself another drink, his face seemingly expressionless.

"You know," said Robert D., "I think you're right. 'Course, it's possible that Sneed has talked to some of the

26

others about us. 'Specially that third one over there. The one they're sitting with."

"So I was wrong," said Pawnee. "It's just them three so far — probably."

"Let's go," said Robert D.

They left the saloon and went back over to the hotel. Purlie was no longer behind the desk. In his place there was another man, an old man with a bald head and tufts of white hair sticking out around his ears. The old man looked up from his reading when he heard the two men come in at the front door.

"Good evening," he said. "Can I help you?"

"No, thanks, pop," said Robert D., holding up his room key. "We're just turning in for the night."

"Oh, you must be the folks that checked in this afternoon."

"That's right."

"Well, good night to you then."

They went up the stairs and unlocked the room in which they had left Trish. Robert D. moved quietly over to the bed to check on her, then he moved as quietly again back out into the hallway, shut the door, and relocked it.

"Sleeping like a baby," he said.

"Good," said Pawnee.

Robert D. looked around. The hallway in which they stood led to the front of the building. There was a window there overlooking Main Street. He motioned for Pawnee to follow him, and they walked down to the window. As he had hoped, the window provided them with a good view of the front of the Tanglefoot.

"Check the back," he said to Pawnee. "See if we can get out of here that way without being seen."

Leaving Robert D. to watch the Tanglefoot from the upstairs hall window, Pawnee moved quickly down the hall to the back of the building. Beyond the last room on his left, Pawnee found that the hallway made a hard left turn and ran all the way to the corner of the building. At that end of the hallway was a door. He tried the door and found it unlocked. Outside was a small landing with a

27

stairway leading down the side wall at the back. He stepped back inside, closed the doors and hurried back to report to Robert D.

"Fire escape," he said.

"Good."

They watched out the window in silence for a few more moments. New customers went into the Tanglefoot. A few left.

"Pawnee," Robert D. said, breaking the silence, "if we get the chance we're looking for, it's got to be done clean and quiet."

"I know."

Pawnee suddenly put a hand on Robert D.'s arm.

"Look," he said.

Down below, the three deputies were coming out of the Tanglefoot together. They turned to their left on the sidewalk and continued walking.

"We going after them?" asked Pawnee.

"Wait," said Robert D.

The deputies stopped at the hitch rail just a couple of doors down from the saloon, where three saddled horses waited. They mounted up and started to ride off in the same direction in which they had been walking.

"Now," said Robert D.

The two hurried to the back door that Pawnee had discovered earlier and rushed down the outside stairs. Robert D. led the way alongside the back of the hotel. At the end of the block, they turned and made their way back to Main Street. They could see the deputies up ahead, still riding, just leaving town.

"Now, where could they be going this time of night?" asked Robert D.

"We get our horses and follow them?" suggested Pawnee.

"Not *our* horses," said Robert D. He looked across the street. Near where the three lawmen had tied their horses others were waiting, their owners probably in the Tanglefoot getting drunk. "A couple of those over there. Can you bring them here without getting caught?"

"I've never yet been caught stealing a horse," said Pawnee.

"Just *borrow* these," said Robert D.

Pawnee studied the street. No one was out just then. He pulled his hat down tight on his forehead, ducked his head, crouched, and ran. Across the street, he quickly unwrapped the reins of two fairly good-looking horses, looked around again, then, walking between the captured mounts, led them across the street to where Robert D. waited.

"Good work," said Robert D. as he swung into the saddle.

Pawnee mounted the other horse, and again Robert D. led the way back behind the buildings. They rode out of town that way, the back way, and they were sure that no one had seen them. The old clerk had seen them go into the hotel for the night, and they had not been seen leaving again. Their own horses were in the stable. If they were careful and if their luck held, it would appear as if they had never left the hotel that night, much less followed three deputies out of town. The deputies were somewhere on the road up ahead. Something had to be out there somewhere. There had to be a reason for them to head out of town together late at night.

"Go slow, Pawnee. We don't want to ride up on them before we know it," said Robert D. Pawnee eased out just slightly ahead of Robert D. The older man let him do it. Nothing had been said about it, but they both knew that Pawnee's senses were keener than those of his companion—his night vision, his hearing, his uncanny sixth sense. They rode like that for perhaps a mile. Then Pawnee reined in his mount and held up a hand. Robert D. barely saw the hand raised in the dark night. He stopped and waited for Pawnee's next move.

"They've stopped," said Pawnee, his voice low, barely audible. "Not far ahead."

He urged his mount forward slowly and Robert D. followed. The ground was almost flat, but where they rode was a slight rise. As they topped the rise, a light became

29

visible to them up ahead. They rode a little farther, until they had come within a hundred yards of the light. They could see then that the light was coming from inside a small building, a house maybe, or a roadside inn. Pawnee signaled for another halt.

"They're in there, I think," he said.

Robert D. dismounted. There didn't seem to be anything around to tie the horses to, so he let the reins trail on the ground.

"All right," he said. "Let's go."

Pawnee swung down out of the saddle, dropping silently to the ground. He twisted his right wrist and pulled out one of the big Remingtons. Robert D. drew his Colt, and they started moving toward the building. As they got closer, they moved more slowly, more cautiously. Soon they could see the three horses the deputies had ridden waiting in front of the small house. There were signs on the front of the building, but in the darkness the lettering was not clear. They eased up to a side window, one on each side, pressed against the wall, and they peered inside. The place was some kind of a country store. It was filled with shelves that contained all kinds of merchandise. A man, maybe forty, was sitting in a straight chair. A woman about the same age stood behind him. Both appeared to be tense, frightened. Over against the far wall one of the deputies lounged and smirked. Warren Sneed stood in front of the man, his arms crossed on his chest. The third deputy was not visible to Pawnee and Robert D. through the window. The window was opened a few inches from the bottom, and the voices from inside were clear to the two spies.

"We don't live in your town," said the man. His voice was determined, yet it quavered. "We don't do business there."

"Sheriff Brody's got jurisdiction over the entire county," said Sneed. "You got to pay your taxes like everyone else. And if you want police protection, you got to pay for that, too."

"We don't want it," said the woman.

"This territory hasn't even been divided into counties," said the man. "You can't say you have jurisdiction out here."

"There was a law passed in Drago at the last town meeting," said Sneed with an exasperated sigh. "The county line has been drawed and you're inside it."

"That's not legal," said the woman.

"Even if it was," said the man, "you don't patrol out here. How would you provide us with protection if you're not ever out here?"

Sneed pulled out one of his Colts and touched the end of its barrel to the tip of the man's nose.

"Something could happen way out here," he said, "that if you had paid for protection, it wouldn't have happened. We'll give you an example. Show them, boys."

The deputy lounging against the far wall made a sudden sweep with his arm and cleaned off the top of the nearby shelf. There was a crash just on the other side of the wall from where Pawnee stood. The third deputy had given away his position. He must have been just there, just across the wall from Pawnee. Pawnee looked at Robert D. The older man gave him a nod, and the two of them ran around to the front door. Pawnee was the first inside, and he jumped immediately to his left. Robert D. came in right behind him. Sneed, his Colt already in hand, whirled around. He just had time to recognize Robert D, and his face registered surprise. Robert D.'s Colt barked, and a bullet smashed into Sneed's sternum. Sneed staggered backward a few steps from the impact of the bullet, then went limp and slumped forward, his face smacking against the hardwood floor with a sickening sound. The other two deputies reached for their guns. Pawnee fired to his own right across the room in front of Robert D. His first shot hit Beeler in the stomach. Beeler made a lurching motion and a sound that gave the impression he was about to puke. Pawnee's second shot caught him in the chest and knocked him back against the wall. Beeler died on his feet, and his lifeless body slid down the wall to crumple up in a grotesque wad. Meantime, Robert D. had turned his atten-

31

tion to the deputy on the other side of the room, who had also drawn his pistol. Robert D. was spinning when he fired, so his shot was a little off. It hit the man in the side of the head, smashing his jaw and tearing out teeth. He fired a second shot into the man's chest. There was a long and eerie pause while the smoke cleared and the ringing left the ears of the four people in the small room. Then the woman stepped up close to the back of the man and put her hands on his shoulders. She stared at the two deadly strangers there before her.

"My God," she said. "Who are you?"

Chapter 4

"I'm Robert D. Wade. This is my partner, Pawnee O'Rourke."

The man got up from his chair. He stood for a moment looking at the three bodies on his floor and at the mess they had made before they had been so abruptly interrupted. He took a deep breath to steady his nerves, then stepped forward to shake Robert D.'s hand.

"Mr. Wade," he said, "my name is Henry Van Tuyl. Everyone calls me Dutch. This is my wife, Lisa."

Robert D. shook Van Tuyl's hand, then Van Tuyl turned toward Pawnee and the scout shook his hand. Mrs. Van Tuyl stepped forward.

"We're grateful to you," she said. "But why? Where did you come from?"

"I'm afraid we don't have time for explanations just now," said Robert D. "For a while at least, we'd prefer that Brody and his men not know what we're up to. We've got two borrowed horses outside, and we need to get them back to town, hopefully before they've been missed by anyone. We also need to move these bodies. We don't want you folks to get the blame for this."

"Can we help?" asked Van Tuyl.

"Yes," said Robert D. "We'll come back tomorrow and explain some things. Maybe you can answer some questions for us, too."

Robert D., Pawnee, and Van Tuyl dragged the bodies out the front door, while Mrs. Van Tuyl started to clean up the mess inside. Van Tuyl hitched a team to a wagon, and they threw the bodies into the back.

"You get the horses back," said Van Tuyl. "I'll take care of these."

Robert D. and Pawnee replaced the two horses at the hitch rail back in town and got back inside the hotel the same way they had left it earlier. No one saw them. Robert D. took out his key and opened the door to Trish's room. She was still asleep, so he locked her back in. Pawnee was at the hall window. When he saw that Robert D. had come back out into the hallway, he motioned toward him to come over to the window. As Robert D. approached, Pawnee gestured with his chin toward the street below. Robert D. looked down. Two cowboys, more than a little drunk, were engaged in a heated discussion with two uniformed deputies. Robert D. raised the window slightly in hopes that the voices might carry across the street. They did.

"I thought you said your damn horses was stole," said one of the deputies.

"They was," said a cowboy.

"Them two right there is yours, ain't they?"

"Well, yeah."

"Well then, by God, they ain't stole."

"Well, they was," said the cowboy.

"You just get on them and go on home," said the deputy, "before I decide to throw you in jail for drunk and disruptive."

Robert D. pushed down the window and chuckled softly. Pawnee grinned.

"Let's turn in," said Robert D., and he walked down the hall to the room next to Trish's and unlocked the door. "We've done a good day's work."

Pawnee nodded.

"I'd call it that," he said.

* * *

Trish was up and dressed early the next morning. She went out into the hall and listened for a moment at the door to Robert D. and Pawnee's room, but she heard no sounds from in there. Thinking that they might have gotten up and out earlier, she went downstairs. She didn't see them there, either. Purlie was behind the desk. She turned to him.

"Have my uncle and our friend come downstairs yet?" she asked.

"No, ma'am," said Purlie. "At least not since I've been here."

"Thanks."

She went back up the stairs and pounded on the door. She heard a groan from inside the room, and she pounded again.

"Uncle Bob," she said. "Pawnee."

"Yeah," came a voice from in the room. She couldn't tell to whom the voice belonged. It was grumpy and full of sleep.

"Come on, you two," she called. "It's well past daybreak."

Pawnee, in his long underwear, opened the door. His eyes were mere slits. When he recognized Trish, he stepped back into the room. She followed him. Robert D. rolled over in the bed.

"Morning, doll," he said.

"You two must be getting old," she said. "I'm up and dressed and ready to go. And I'm hungry as a bear come spring. Come on. Get up."

Robert D. threw back the covers and swung his legs around to sit up on the edge of the bed and rub his eyes.

"You're right," he said. "I'm getting old."

Pawnee found his britches and was pulling them on one leg.

"Ain't we all," he said. "Ain't we all."

They went back to Maude's for breakfast, but this time

they found the small cafe full of customers. Claude was too busy to engage in idle conversation. The food was still fine, though, and besides, Robert D. didn't really want to talk to Claude anymore. It didn't seem like a good idea to ask too many questions of the same people. He still wanted to maintain the image that he and his two partners were just casual visitors to Drago. Too many questions, especially too many in the same place, would give them away as investigators. They finished their breakfasts and left Maude's. Standing out on the sidewalk, Trish asked, "What now?"

"Let's go down to the livery stable and get our horses," said Robert D. "We got some folks we'd like you to meet."

Trish gave Robert D. a puzzled look. Robert D.'s expression didn't change. He started walking down the street toward the livery stable. Trish turned an enquiring face toward Pawnee. He smiled at her, a silly smile, she thought. Robert D. continued on his way to the livery stable without looking back, and Pawnee hurried ahead to catch up with him. He fell in step just to Robert D.'s left. Trish stared after them for a moment, her hands on her hips. They didn't know anyone in Drago, and she had been with them everywhere they went. How could they have some folks they wanted her to meet? She had let them get ahead of her, so she had to run to catch up. She forced her way in between the two of them.

"Tell me what's going on," she said to Robert D. He didn't answer. He just kept walking. She turned to Pawnee.

"What the hell are you two up to?" she asked. Pawnee gave no response. Trish kept walking along between the two men, turning her head from one to the other with questions all the way to the livery stable. Only when they had arrived within earshot of the stableman did she stop her questions. She waited, huffy, her arms crossed over her round breasts, while the horses were being saddled. Then they mounted up, and Robert D. led the way out of town.

"Trish, this is Dutch Van Tuyl and his wife, Lisa. This

36

here is Trish. She's my . . . well, her older brother was my godson, and I've kind of raised her since she lost her parents."

"How do you do?" said Dutch.

"We're very pleased to meet you," said Lisa. "Your . . . uh . . ."

Lisa was looking at Robert D. and searching for the right words. Trish understood her dilemma and decided to help her out.

"I call him Uncle Bob," she said.

"Your Uncle Bob and Mr. O'Rourke did us a great favor last night."

"I'd like to hear about that," said Trish, shooting a dirty look at Robert D.

"Three of Brody's men came out here demanding tax payment and protection money," said Dutch. "We refused to pay. They were just starting to bust up the place when these two jumped in and stopped them."

"Did you have any trouble disposing of the . . . uh . . . evidence?" asked Robert D.

"Not a bit," said Dutch. "I dumped them clean out on the other side of town, out beyond Brody's house. No one will ever even guess that they came from over this direction. How about you and the horses?"

"We got them returned with no problem," said Robert D. "Just a little embarrassment to their owners."

Pawnee chuckled from where he stood over in a corner of the room. Trish placed her hands on her hips and gave her two companions a stern frown.

"And I thought you two had just passed out last night," she said. "Well, what do we do now?"

"We still need to know a little more about what we're up against," said Robert D., "before we can make any plans."

"If you don't mind me butting in," said Dutch, "what is it you need to know? Maybe we can help."

Robert D. gave Dutch a hard look. Then he looked at Lisa, and finally at each of his partners. He rubbed his stubble-covered chin.

"I think we just as well tell these folks everything," he

said. "We could sure use some local allies."

Pawnee nodded in silent assent.

"Whatever you think, Uncle Bob," said Trish.

"Can we all sit down some place and talk?" asked Robert D.

"Sure," said Lisa. "Follow me."

She led them into a back room, which apparently served as the dining room for the Van Tuyls. There were other rooms behind the store, indicating that the Van Tuyls had their living quarters in the same building as their place of business. They all sat down around the table, and Lisa offered coffee. When she had everyone provided with a cup, she sat down with them. Robert D. took a sip.

"Trish here," he said, "is Trish Madison."

He paused, waiting to see if the Madison name got any reaction out of the Van Tuyls. Lisa just sat and waited for Robert D. to say something more, without giving any indication that the name had meant anything to her. Dutch furrowed his brow a bit. The name had struck a chord with him, but he didn't want to comment until he had heard further information.

"Bobby was her older brother," said Robert D. "He was my godson."

"Bobby Madison," said Dutch. "The man who was killed by Brody. This is all beginning to make some sense."

"That's right," said Robert D.

"And that's not the worst of it," said Trish. "If Bobby had been all those things they say he was, and if it had happened the way they say it did, we wouldn't be here. As much as I loved Bobby, if all that was true, I'd let it go. But it's not true."

"This here rag," said Robert D., pulling the book he had purchased from Claude out of his back pocket and tossing it onto the center of the table, "describes a gunfight out in the middle of the street in broad daylight. I can't find out that anybody in Drago actually saw that gunfight."

"And you won't, either," said Dutch. "Brody shot Bobby Madison in the back late one night in the Tanglefoot Saloon."

Trish almost came up out of her chair.

"How do you know that?" she asked.

"There are a few people in Drago who will still talk — at least to each other — when there's no one around to eavesdrop. I talked to a man who was there when it happened."

"We suspected as much," said Robert D. "It's good to have it confirmed."

"So you came here to kill Brody," said Dutch.

"If there was any real law around here," said Robert D., "we'd try to see that justice was done proper. We'd let the law handle it. But there ain't. When you can't get justice, revenge will have to do."

Dutch leaned back in his chair with a loud sigh. He pulled out a pouch of Bull Durham from his pocket, removed paper, and began to fashion himself a smoke. When he had licked it and stuck it between his lips, he held the pouch out toward Robert D.

"Thanks. I will," said Robert D.

Dutch tossed the makings across the table, then reached back into his pocket for a wooden match. He struck the match on the bottom of the table and lit his cigarette. He pulled out another match and tossed it over to Robert D.

"You'll have to fight his whole army," he said. "He won't be an easy target."

"How many?" asked Pawnee.

"There were twelve," said Dutch. "You took out three last night. That leaves nine. Nine deputies and Brody."

"Nine against three," said Trish. "That's not so bad."

Robert D. passed the Bull Durham on to Pawnee, who set about making himself a smoke. Robert D. lit his, took a deep drag, and expelled the smoke.

"We saw two of them in Brody's backyard yesterday," he said. "Are they always there?"

"Yeah," said Dutch. "He keeps them there when he's home as bodyguards. When he's not home, they just guard the house, I guess. That is, until they started selling tickets to the — to the grave."

"He keeps them there to watch her," said Lisa. "His wife. Susan. From what I hear, she bears watching."

39

"Oh, yeah . . . well," said Dutch, "there's that, too."

"Oh?" said Robert D., raising his eyebrows. "Mrs. Brody is a—"

"—trollop," said Lisa.

"That's interesting," said Robert D. "Where do the other seven deputies hang around?"

"There's usually two or three of them in the Tanglefoot," said Dutch, "depending on how busy it is. That's Brody's own establishment. The others could be anywhere—patrolling the streets, collecting blood money. You never know."

Pawnee sucked on his cigarette, looking thoughtful.

"That's two at the house," he said. "Say two in the Tanglefoot. There's five out loose somewhere. And then there's Brody."

Trish appeared to be getting more and more nervous during this conversation. She reached for the makings that Pawnee had left on the table in front of himself and began to roll herself a cigarette. Lisa Van Tuyl gave her a disapproving look.

"Somebody said that Brody's off at the capitol," said Robert D. "Said he'd be back for the celebration. Is there a way we could catch him somewhere along the road?"

"Not without knowing exactly how and when he's coming back," said Dutch. "Even if he rode the stage, there are several different times he could be coming in. And I don't know if he rode the stage or not. He might be horseback, or he might've taken his own buggy. He could have taken some deputies with him. Probably did. I just don't know."

"So while he's away," said Trish, "there's just the two guards at the house and Mrs. Brody inside. Right?"

"And the big dog," said Dutch.

"Big dog? What kind of big dog?" asked Pawnee.

"I don't know what kind," said Dutch, "but it's a vicious one. Even the deputies are afraid of it. No one can get near it except Brody himself and Susan Brody."

"We didn't see anything of a dog," said Trish.

"He's inside most of the time with Susan. They only bring him out on a leash. That little fence around the backyard wouldn't hold him in, and he's too dangerous to let loose."

Robert D. stood up and paced the floor away from the table. He was thoughtfully rubbing at the stubble on his chin. He took a final drag on his cigarette, turned back to the table, and snubbed it out in an ashtray.

"One final question," he said. "If Brody and his deputies were out of the way, would anyone else in Drago block our path?"

"If you get rid of Brody and his bunch," said Dutch, "they'll likely give the whole town to you. There may even be a few brave enough to help you along the way. But for sure, no one will interfere."

Chapter 5

There was a fair-sized crowd of tourists at the gate of the backyard, clamoring to get in to see the grave of Bobby Madison. Robert D. was grateful for that. It kept the two guards occupied while he walked around to the front of the big blue house. He stepped up onto the porch and knocked on the door. With the first sound of his fist, a mighty roar came from inside the house. The barking was so loud and sudden that Robert D. actually flinched and felt a skip in his heartbeat. Then the door was opened a crack, and the vicious barking grew even louder. Robert D. could see through the crack the snarling, slavering fangs of the monster dog. He forced himself to look away from the beast to the face of the woman who held it back. She spoke to him, but he could not understand her words over the din created by the dog. When he spoke, he raised his voice to almost a yell.

"Mrs. Brody?" he shouted. "I'm Robert D. Wade. Is your husband at home?"

"No," shouted the woman. "He's out of town."

"I've come a long ways to see him," said Robert D., still shouting over the barks and snarls of the beast. "Can you tell me when he might be back? When I might be able to see him?"

"What?" asked Mrs. Brody. "Wait a minute. Just let me put General away."

She shut the door, leaving Robert D. standing on the porch. He looked around to see if anyone was watching, if anyone saw him at the Brody house. No one seemed to notice. He thought that he was safe so far. Soon the barking subsided, and in another moment, Mrs. Brody again opened the door. This time she opened it fully.

"I'm sorry about General," she said, "but my husband is away just now. A woman alone can't be too careful, you know. What did you say your name is?"

"I'm Robert D. Wade, ma'am. I was hoping to see your husband."

Of course, Robert D. was lying. He knew that Brody was out of town, and that was the reason he had gone to the blue house. Susan Brody cocked her head to one side and studied Robert D. Her lips formed a half smile. A good-looking woman, thought Robert D. Not bad at all. Susan Brody stepped to one side.

"Won't you come in, Mr. Wade?" she said.

Robert D. took off his hat and stepped inside the big blue house. He pulled the door closed behind him. A woman alone can't be too careful, huh? he thought. Then why has she let me in with the dog made safe in another room? And she's got those two armed guards just out in the yard out back.

"Thank you, ma'am," he said. "As I was saying, I came a long ways to see your husband. I—"

"He'll be back tomorrow," said Mrs. Brody, interrupting Robert D., "or the next day. Will you be in town that long?"

"Well, I . . . uh . . . I expect I can hang around until he gets back."

"May I ask what business you have with my husband?"

"Well, none, really," said Robert D. "I was a soldier by trade. I've had nothing but odd jobs since the war. I heard that I might be useful to Mr. Brody down here in Drago."

"So you're looking for work? You have the look of a man who can handle those guns you wear. Have you ever killed a man, Mr. Wade?"

Robert D. ducked his head, as if the answer to that

question was an embarrassment. He still held his hat in front of him in both hands.

"I . . . uh . . . well, yes, ma'am, I have," he said. "A few times."

"A few times," said Mrs. Brody. "Well. But would you please stop calling me ma'am? Call me Susan. And what may I call you? Must I continue calling you Mr. Wade?"

"My friends mostly call me Robert D. I'm not sure just where or when that got started."

"I like that, Robert D.," said Susan. "Please sit down. May I get you a drink? I have some very nice sherry. Or would you prefer something stronger? I imagine you would."

"I like a good brown whiskey," said Robert D. "Thanks."

Susan walked to a nearby liquor cabinet. She took out a glass and then a bottle of whiskey, and poured it full for Robert D. Then she poured herself a sherry. She carried the drinks back across the room. Robert D. stood up as she handed him the whiskey, and Susan held out her glass as if for a toast. He awkwardly clinked his glass against hers.

"Here's to your health, Robert D.," she said.

"And yours," he said, and took a good hearty slug of whiskey from the glass.

"Sit down," she said.

Robert D. started to sit back down in the chair he had taken before, but she stopped him.

"Over here," she said. "Please."

She had moved to a short velvet-covered divan, toward which she made a sweeping gesture with her left arm. Robert D. walked to the divan and sat down. Susan sat beside him.

"That's a hell of a big dog you've got back there, Mrs. . . . uh . . . excuse me, Susan," said Robert D. "What did you call him? General?"

"His full name is General Beauregard. We call him General for short."

"What kind is he?"

"Do you like dogs, Robert D.?"

"Well, yes, I kind of do. I get along pretty well with most all animals, except sometimes the human kind."

"Well," said Susan, "don't try to get friendly with General. He'll tear you to pieces. My husband trained him that way. He's half bloodhound and half mastiff. Why do you want to work for my husband?"

"I just want work," said Robert D. "There's not much available."

Susan sipped at her sherry and looked over the top of her glass at Robert D. Her eyes looked hungry, he thought. There was a strange longing there, a longing and a kind of desperation. What was this woman up to? And why had she invited him in and offered him a drink?

"Are you very particular, Robert D.," she asked, "about the kind of man you work for or the kind of work you do?"

"What do you mean?"

"If you work for my husband, you'll have to steal and murder. That's his business."

Robert D. tossed down the rest of his whiskey, put the glass down, and stood up. He gave Susan a hard look.

"Do you interview everyone who applies for a job with your husband?" he asked. "I won't fall into your trap."

He turned and headed toward the front door, as if to leave. Susan jumped to her feet and followed him.

"Wait," she said. "Don't go. Listen to me. I'm serious. What do you know about Sheriff Phil Brody? Anything? He rules this town and everyone in it with an iron fist."

"Does that include you, Susan?" asked Robert D.

"Yes," she said, and for the first time, her eyes were not able to meet his gaze. She looked at the floor. "When he can."

"Why are you telling me all this?"

"Because I want to know just what you are capable of, Robert D. Just how far will you go for money?"

Robert D. walked back to the velvet-covered divan and sat down.

"Suppose you tell me just what it is you've got in mind," he said.

45

"If Phil gives you a job, you'll get a fair salary, but you'll never get rich and you'll never be your own boss," said Susan, quickly rejoining Robert D. on the divan. "I've got a proposition that will make you rich."

"I'm listening."

Susan set her wine glass down and leaned toward Robert D.

"Look at me," she said. "Do you like what you see?"

"I like it," said Robert D., and he wasn't lying. But she was another man's wife and that went against his grain, and he had more important things on his mind than dallying anyway. In addition, he had a strong feeling that this was a devious woman, one who could not be trusted. Yet she was very tempting, leaning forward toward him there on the velvet divan, her eyes half closed, her lips parted slightly, the tip of her wet tongue showing against the back of her white teeth. Her neck and shoulders were bare, and in the posture she had assumed, the cleavage between her fulsome breasts looked inviting. She reached out with her left arm and caught Robert D. behind the head. She pulled him toward her as she leaned in further, and her open lips met his in a warm, wet, deep kiss. Robert D. felt a serious stirring deep within, and he knew that this would lead to no good. Susan backed off from the kiss.

"Robert D.," she said, "I'm a slave here. I want out. If you kill my husband, I'll inherit everything. You can have me and the money. You can take over Drago if you want, or we can take the money and go away someplace."

"I don't know," said Robert D. "He's got all those deputies."

"I can help you. I can tell you things. Besides, there are only nine of them now. Three of them were killed yesterday outside of town. No one knows who did it. Robert D., we can do it together. At least think about it."

"I'm thinking," said Robert D.

"There are only nine," she said, "but there are four more on the way. Phil hired them by mail or telegram or something. Professional killers. They're on the way right now. You see, you need me, Robert D."

46

She reached around his body with both arms and pulled herself close to him. Her lips nibbled at his neck and ears until they finally found their way back to his mouth. In his mind, Robert D. tried to fight the powerful urge. Then he thought, it's all for a good reason, and finally, aw, the hell with it. He turned his body slightly, allowing Susan to lower herself onto her back on the soft velvet divan.

"Where the hell have you been?" asked Trish. "We've been trying to decide whether or not we should charge that big house, guns ablazing."

"I'm glad you decided to wait," said Robert D.

"Well," asked Trish, "what have you been doing in there?"

"I've been . . . uh . . . talking to Mrs. Brody," he said. "Checking things out. She does have a vicious dog, half bloodhound, half mastiff. His name's General Beauregard."

"I can handle dogs," said Pawnee.

"You don't want to try to handle this one," said Robert D. "It's a trained killer. Anyhow, Susan . . . uh . . . that is, Mrs. Brody is afraid of her husband. She feels like she's a captive in that house, and she wants out. She wants me to kill him for her, and she said she'd help. I told her to use her influence with him, if she's got any, to get me a deputy's job. Brody's coming back to town tomorrow, according to her."

"Robert D.," said Pawnee, "that woman might be setting you up for some kind of trap. You think about that?"

"I thought about it, Pawnee. I thought about it real hard, and I think she's playing it straight with me. She wants her freedom. She might shoot me in the back once I get her out, but up until then, I think she's straight. She wants my help, and to get it, she'll help me. And that means she'll be helping us. I mean to play the hand out."

"What can she do for us anyhow?" asked Trish.

"For one thing, she can control that dog. She can also give us information about the movements of Brody and his deputies. He likely don't tell her all his plans, but she'll hear some things. We need a way in that big house, and she can let me in. She'll be a good ally, Trish. Trust me on this."

Trish stalked away from Robert D., a pouty expression on her face. She crossed her arms over her breasts, then turned back to face him again.

"Me and Pawnee are hungry," she said. "We didn't eat lunch. We were just waiting for you to get back. Let's go eat somewhere."

"Good idea," said Robert D. "For some reason, I got a powerful hunger myself. Where do you want to go? Back to Maude's?"

"Yeah," said Pawnee. "I'm getting kind of fond of her cooking."

"Oh. Do I need to warn Claude about this?" asked Robert D.

"All I want's her cooking," said Pawnee, "and I don't reckon that matters much to Claude, as long as he collects for it."

Trish snorted and hurried on ahead of her companions.

Back in the blue house, Susan Brody sat alone on the divan. Her dress was badly rumpled and her underthings were scattered on the floor at her bare feet. She stared across the room at the wall before her with a blank expression on her face, and she recalled the last time Phil Brody had beat her. She recalled it vividly. He had accused her of having had an affair with a handsome young deputy of his. Of course, she had thought about it, had fantasized, had even longed to find a way to get the young man alone, but it had never happened. Phil hadn't believed her, though, and he had beaten her for her imagined transgression. Then she thought of Robert D. Wade. If anyone could kill Phil Brody, Robert D. was the man. If anyone could get through the small army of deputies to accomplish that task, she felt sure it would be he. She had a strong feeling about that. There was something about the

48

man. There was something in his cold gray eyes, in the hard lines of his face and the hardness of his body. There was also something about the ease with which he strapped on his six-gun and the comfort with which he carried it. And he moved like a wild animal, she thought. She longed to watch him kill Phil Brody. She wanted her freedom, yes, but she wanted more than that. She wanted her revenge.

Susan stood up and walked to a door at the back of the room. She opened the door, and General came rushing out. He ran to the front door and sniffed, then to the divan. He rushed from one corner of the room to another, smelling out all the places in his home the stranger had been. Susan went back to the divan and sat down again. Finally, General, realizing that the intruder was gone, trotted up to her, his great tongue lapping out of his mouth and dripping saliva. She held out a hand to him, and he nuzzled his great head onto her lap. Slowly, absentmindedly, Susan scratched his huge head between the ears.

Chapter 6

They had finished their meal, and Trish was still pouting at Robert D. She didn't believe for a minute that he had spent all that time talking to Susan Brody. Talking indeed, she thought. In a corner of her brain, she chastised herself for feeling like that. He was a man, after all, and he had his . . . well, his needs. But the wife of Phil Brody. Damn.

Robert D. leaned across the table toward Trish and spoke in a low voice.

"So you don't think we need Susan Brody," he said.

"No," said Trish. She didn't look at Robert D.

"Well," he said, "we've got a job to do."

"Now?" said Pawnee.

"Right now."

"What is it?" Trish asked. "Is it something she told you?"

"Clay Meredith," said Robert D. "Hock Snyder. Cholly Ingalls. Skeeter Bowls."

"What about them?" asked Pawnee.

"Who are they?" questioned Trish.

"They're a bunch of rattlesnakes," said Pawnee. "Gunslingers. Every one of them wanted for murder. More than once and in more than one state.

"The very bunch I'm talking about," said Robert D. "Brody has been in touch with them. He's been wanting to beef up his little army here, and those four are on the way."

"Well, what are we going to do?" asked Trish, forgetting her pout.

"We can't afford to let them get to town," said Robert D. "We already have more than enough to handle here. If we can stop them before they get to Drago, we'll accomplish two things. First, we keep the size of the army down here in town. Second, we make it easier to approach Brody as replacements. He'll be worried if his four killers don't show."

"So, how do we know where and when to look for these guys?" asked Trish.

"They're due in here tonight," said Robert D., "and they'll be riding in horseback coming south on the main road."

"How did you find out all that?" asked Trish.

Robert D. simply raised his eyebrows and gave Trish a look. In response, she lowered her eyes.

"Oh, yeah," she said. "Susan . . . Brody." The last name was pronounced with bitterness. She looked up again quickly, though with a new thought.

"So what do we do?" she asked. "Jump the first four men we see coming down the road? There's people pouring into this town."

Robert D. and Pawnee looked into each other's eyes. Their looks were cold and hard.

"We know this bunch," said Pawnee.

"Let's get going then," said Robert D.

Four hard-looking men were on the road. They traveled abreast, each one looking straight ahead. Each one had a blanket roll behind his saddle and a rifle in a saddle boot. They sat on tough, rangy cow ponies, and horses and men alike showed signs of a long and rugged trip. The man on the right was Clay Meredith. Cleaned up and shaved, he would probably have been a handsome man. About thirty years old, he had steel blue eyes and sandy hair. His beard was ragged, a trail beard. Likely he would shave it off

51

when he reached town. His clothes, though dirty and wrinkled from travel, were expensive and tasteful, and he wore high-topped quality leather boots. He wore two holstered .45 Colts on his thighs.

To his left rode Hock Snyder, a small man, an albino with shoulder-length white hair and watery, colorless eyes. He was thin-lipped, with gaunt features and a hungry look. His clothes were all black, making him a study in contrast. He, too, wore a pair of Colts, but his were worn high, the reversed butts tilted inward almost on his rib cage for a cross draw. Next to him was Cholly Ingalls, tall and slim with a handlebar mustache, drooping now from lack of attention on the trail. Ingalls wore a three-piece suit. The jacket lay across the saddle in front of him. He carried two .38 caliber Smith and Wesson revolvers in special made holster-pockets on the vest. He did not wear boots but wore high-topped shoes with spats. On the far left was Skeeter Bowls. Bowls was a man with no apparent concern for his appearance. His general demeanor was slovenly, his skin greasy, and his equally greasy hair hung in long rattails down around his pinched face. His beard was straggly. His first stop in town would most likely be for whiskey, not for a bath and a shave.

They did not ride together like friends. They did not chat or smile or even look at one another. They rode instead with near military precision, yet it was a casual precision. No one was in charge. There were no commands. They were four individuals with a single goal and purpose. And when they saw the mounted man in the road ahead, just sitting there, waiting, facing them, they stopped together. They looked at the man for at least a full minute, and without ever a glance at each other, they urged their mounts forward at a slow walk—together. As they drew closer to the waiting man, they all recognized him. He was a man they had all known at different times in their lives, in different places. They recognized him, yet still they did not speak to each other, did not glance at each other. They rode ahead steadily. The man waiting for them there in the road ahead did not move. He sat on his horse and watched as the four riders approached. When they had arrived within ten feet of where he sat, they stopped, again as a unit. They looked at him, and he returned their steady gaze. There was a long moment of silence before Clay Meredith spoke.

"Robert D. Wade," he said.

Robert D. gave a curt nod.

"Hello, Clay," he said.

"It's been a long time, Robert D."

"Not long enough."

"That's just the way I feel about it," said Bowls. "What the hell you doing here?"

"Waiting for you," said Robert D. "Isn't that obvious?"

"All right," said Meredith. "We're here. What do you want?"

"I want you to turn around and ride out of here," said Robert D.

"Why would we want to do that?" asked Ingalls.

"It's been a long ride, Robert D.," said Meredith, "and it's a hell of a ride back to the nearest town. I need a a bath and a nice soft bed."

"I'm looking forward to a good steak dinner," said Ingalls.

"A woman," said Snyder.

"And whiskey," said Bowls.

"You won't like Drago," said Robert D. "It's getting crowded. You'll have to wait in line for all that stuff. It's a long ride back, but the service will be better when you get there."

"We're going to Drago," said Meredith.

"We got jobs," said Bowls.

"I know all about your jobs," said Robert D. "You can get jobs somewhere else. Why don't you just turn around and head back? I got no quarrel with you men. Not just now."

Ingalls leaned forward, resting a forearm on his saddle horn, and squinted at Robert D.

"What's your stake in this anyhow, Wade?" he asked.

"I've got business with Phil Brody," said Robert D.

"You'd just get in the way."

"What kind of business?" asked Bowls.

"I aim to kill him," said Robert D. "Him and anybody that's hired on to protect him. I'm giving you notice. Fair warning."

"Notice is taken, Robert D.," said Meredith. "We appreciate the courtesy. But now if you'll just move out of our way, we're riding on into town."

"No, you're not," said Robert D.

Meredith smiled for the first time, and for the first time he glanced at his three companions. Then he looked back at Robert D.

"That's pretty bold talk," he said. "You planning to stop all four of us? Just you?"

"Not just me," said Robert D.

From off to the side of the road, behind Meredith and to his right, Pawnee O'Rourke stepped out from behind a clump of brush. He held his Winchester in his hands and he chambered a shell. The sound stiffened the four gunfighters.

"I'm here, too, boys," said Pawnee.

Meredith turned his head slowly, just enough to look over his shoulder and spot Pawnee.

"O'Rourke," he said. "I should have known he'd be around. So there's two of you."

"Three," said Trish, coming up out of the tall prairie grass to the left. She, too, was behind the riders. She held her .36 Colt in her right hand.

"Two men and a gal," said Ingalls with a sneer.

"If you know anything about us at all," said Robert D., "then you know that gal there can knock off your collar button from where she stands."

" 'Course that means the bullet would have to travel through your neck first to get there," added Pawnee.

"What's it going to be, Clay?" asked Robert D.

Clay Meredith knew that it would be difficult, if not impossible, for Snyder and Ingalls, the two in the middle, to turn and fire at Pawnee and Trish. He would have to go for Pawnee, and Bowls, on the other end, would have to take the girl. That meant that Snyder and Ingalls would have to be responsible for Robert D. Wade. He regretted that situation just a bit. If he had to have a showdown with Robert D. Wade, he would have liked to have it direct, face to face, just the two of them. But Meredith was not too sentimental. He dealt with each situation as it was given, so he would take O'Rourke. He knew that his companions had sized up the situation the same way. He didn't have to tell them what to do, they would just do it. But he also knew that Robert D. Wade had figured it all out the same way. O'Rourke probably had as well. He wasn't sure about the girl, but if Robert D. had trained her, then he had to figure that she, too, was of a like mind. So everyone knew the role he would play in the fight to follow. It would be a real contest of wits and skill. Who was the fastest, the cleverest, the surest shot, the coolest head. It would be a hell of a fight. Too bad there was no audience, no reporter to write it up. Oh, well.

He pulled out his right-hand Colt and flung himself to the left out of the saddle all in one motion. That placed him between his own horse and O'Rourke, who would have picked him for a target. His plan was to keep O'Rourke as his own target while at the same time frustrating Pawnee's aim. If his plan worked, Pawnee would be forced to pick a different target, and the rhythm of O'Rourke, Wade, and the girl would be spoiled. He counted on his own comrades to stick with what he knew were their original plans. But he didn't count on the ability of his enemies to make quick adjustments, and he didn't count on the extra seconds it would take him to aim under the belly of his surprised and fidgeting horse.

Instead of worrying about the two in the middle as Meredith had figured he would, Robert D. simply decided to protect Pawnee from this surprise. He pulled his revolver and sent a shot into Meredith's back, just below the neck and between the shoulders. Because of the angle at which Meredith was lying on the ground, the shot entered and exited through the back, tearing up a couple of vertebrae in its path. At the same time, Pawnee, reacting to the surprise move of his primary target, aimed for his secondary target, Hock Snyder. The lead from the Winchester tore through Snyder's skull, splattering brains over the mane of the albino's horse. Snyder's near-lifeless body jerked and twitched in the saddle, then slumped, sagged, and finally slid off to the right, landing on Meredith, who had fallen back but was still alive. Trish had not waited for anyone to turn and fire at her. As soon as Meredith had made his first move, she shot Bowls in the back. He fell forward to lie as if asleep on his horse's neck. Ingalls had dropped his reins and pulled both pistols from his vest pockets as soon as he had seen Meredith's move, but Robert D., upon firing his first shot, had spurred his horse, causing it to leap forward right at the line of gunfighters. Ingalls's horse reacted with fright, causing Ingalls's first shot to go wild. As Robert D. raced past him, Ingalls twisted in the saddle to follow his prey. As he did, Pawnee fired a second round from the Winchester. The bullet smashed through Ingalls's sternum. He fell backward out of the saddle. Horses stamped and nickered. Pawnee and Trish stood still, surveying the carnage, ready for any unexpected movement. Robert D., having run through the line of horses, turned his own mount back around to face the bodies there on the ground. The fight was over. He holstered his Colt and briefly studied the results of the fight.

"I asked them to leave," he said. "I'll go fetch your horses."

He turned to ride off to the west where they had left the other two animals, and as he turned, Meredith's arm came out from under the body of Snyder. He still held his revolver, and it was already cocked. Meredith raised his head in order to see over the lifeless lump that was pinning him to the ground, and he took aim at Robert D.'s back. Pawnee's view was obscured by the milling horses. Trish saw the movement, but she didn't have a clear shot. She ran toward Meredith and shouted at the same time.

"Uncle Bob," she said. "Watch out."

Robert D. ducked to his right as Meredith pulled the

trigger, and he felt the bullet burn a new scar across his upper arm. He dropped beneath the horse's neck, his Colt once again in his hand, but Trish was already there. He saw her as she stopped, stood coldly still, and sent a bullet into Meredith's head. Pawnee walked forward.

"We better kick them other three just to be damn sure," he said, and in another minute he added, "They're all dead — now. Good work, girl."

"Can I go now?" asked Robert D., feeling slightly embarrassed.

"Go on, Uncle Bob," said Trish. "We've got everything here under control."

The loose horses finally settled down, and Trish and Pawnee, waiting for Robert D. to return with their own mounts, stood in silence looking over the scene.

"Well," said Trish finally, "that's four we won't have to deal with later on."

"Yeah," said Pawnee. "We probably ought to do something with these bodies — and these horses."

"Don't worry," said Trish. "Robert D.'s probably already got something figured out."

Chapter 7

Phil Brody felt good. He felt about as good as he had ever felt in his life. During his almost week-long visit, he had talked to all the right people at the capitol, and he felt sure that he would be appointed the next territorial governor—about as sure as anyone could feel about something like that. What was more, he knew that once he was in that position, once he had become the actual territorial governor, he would be able to do all the right things to delay statehood at least long enough to make himself a millionaire. And if he found that he liked the life of governor, with that kind of money, even after statehood, which, of course, was inevitable, he would certainly be able to manage to get himself elected. He hadn't been sure of all this when he had left Drago to make this trip, but on his way back he was sure. He was damn sure. He knew that he could pull it off.

He was riding a special unscheduled stagecoach, and as an extra precaution, in addition to the driver and the man riding shotgun, there were two heavily armed guards inside the stage with Brody, hired just for this trip. There were no other passengers, and the stage was carrying no freight, just Brody's luggage. He was taking no chances with his own safety. In addition to his sense of elation at his assessment of his own political future, he was also looking forward with great anticipation to the big gala celebration of

Drago's twenty-fifth birthday. Much of the celebration would focus on what Brody, himself, had done for the town, how he had brought law and order and civilization to this raw and wild frontier. Edgar Wilhelm McDowell's fine new book, *Phil Brody, Frontier Lawman: The Man Who Killed Bobby Madison,* would be on display and on sale everywhere in Drago, and people would be guided to the grave site of the notorious killer Madison right there in Brody's own backyard.

McDowell would cover the celebration thoroughly in his newspaper, and he would even send the stories to the big papers in the east. Before it was all over and done, Brody would be a big national hero like Buffalo Bill or Wild Bill Hickok, maybe even bigger. He leaned back in the seat and puffed an expensive cigar. The world looked pretty damn good to Phil Brody.

The stagecoach was unexpected in Drago, so naturally a crowd of the curious gathered around the stage stop to find out what it was all about. They milled about and murmured to themselves and to each other, until the doors opened and the two guards got out, followed by Brody. Most of the crowd dispersed when the sheriff made his appearance. He stepped up onto the sidewalk and started walking toward the Tanglefoot without another word or a look back at the four hirelings who had brought him home. Their job was over, and as far as he was concerned, they had been paid and paid well, so they could go to hell or to Texas. Whichever. He didn't care. When the bartender in the Tanglefoot saw Brody walk in, he took a glass and a bottle of the sheriff's favorite brandy over to the table that was always reserved for him. He poured the first drink, and then he stepped back out of the way. Brody took his seat at the table.

"Welcome home, Mr. Brody," said the bartender. Brody picked up the glass and took a drink. He did not respond to the bartender's greeting. A uniformed deputy stationed across the room had seen Brody come in, and he hurried over to Brody's table.

"Sheriff," he said, "we had some bad trouble while you were gone."

Brody downed the rest of his drink and refilled the glass. Then he glared up at the deputy.

"Damn it," he said. "I just got done with a long and tiring trip. I'd like to be able to relax a little bit before I have to start dealing with problems. Can't anyone around here take care of anything by himself without me having to be right here every minute to tell them every goddamned move to make? Where the hell is Sneed?"

"Well, sir," said the deputy, "that's part of what I'm trying to tell you. Sneed's dead."

"What?"

"Yes, sir. Sneed's dead. Him and Olson and Bass. Shot to death."

Brody's face went white with anger. He turned up his glass and took a big gulp of brandy.

"Who did it?" he demanded.

The deputy shuffled his feet and looked down at the floor. He was not comfortable in the role of the bearer of bad tidings.

"We don't know," he said. "They was found out on the road, the three of them. Just a-laying there. Their horses was found wandering loose not far off, out on the north road just beyond your house."

"So what the hell have you done about it?" asked Brody.

"We talked to people in town. Can't find no one who heard or seen anything. They was in here earlier the same day. Sneed and them, I mean. In here in the Tanglefoot. And they left together that night. It was late. No one knows nothing about them after that. Not 'til we found them dead."

"Someone knows," said Brody. "Someone knows, and we're going to find him. Get everyone in here. Now."

The deputy turned to obey his command, but Brody stopped him abruptly with an afterthought.

"Hold on," he said. "Who's guarding my house?"

"I believe it's Hogan and Sand."

"Get everybody else in here right now," said Brody, "but leave them two right where they're at."

"Yes, sir," said the deputy, and he practically ran out of the Tanglefoot. Brody finished his second glass of brandy and poured himself a third.

"Burl," he shouted. The bartender came running out from behind the bar and over to Brody's table.

"Yes, sir?"

"Send somebody after Ed. Tell him I want to see him."

"Mr. McDowell?" asked Burl the bartender.

"Hell, yes, Mr. McDowell," said Brody. "Ed McDowell. Who else? Get him over here, and hurry up about it."

"Yes, sir," said Burl, hustling away to comply.

In a few moments, Edgar McDowell came strolling in. Burl met him at Brody's table with a glass and another bottle. No one was allowed to drink from Brody's special bottle. Burl left again as quickly as he could.

"Hello, Phil," said McDowell. "How was the trip?"

"Never mind that now," said Brody. "What do you know about these killings?"

"Sneed and them?" asked McDowell. "No one seems to know anything about it. They found the bodies out on the road north of your house. That's all I've heard. Except that they were all shot in the front."

"Well, what the hell are my goddamned deputies doing about it? What do I pay them for?"

"They've been questioning people around town, Phil," said McDowell. "They checked over the ground where the bodies were found. But they are at a dead end, it seems."

"Goddamn it," said Brody, "I can't turn my back for five minutes without something going wrong around here. It looks like I have to be right here all the damn time if I want to maintain any kind of order in this town."

McDowell slapped a hand on Brody's shoulder. Brody was McDowell's new hero, McDowell's creation in a very real sense, and he knew how to manipulate the man, knew what made him tick and knew what it would take to use

61

him for personal profit.

"Phil," he said, "don't be too hard on them. They're just ordinary men. It takes a special man like you to run a town like Drago. That's exactly why you're in the position you're in. That's why you are Phil Brody. No one else. You. Just you. Don't worry. You'll get to the bottom of this."

Brody leaned back in his chair and puffed out his chest. He pulled a fresh cigar out of his coat pocket. McDowell found a match in his own pocket rather quickly, struck it on the underneath side of the tabletop, and held it out for Brody to use to light his cigar. Brody's expression had remained serious, but it was no longer so ireful. McDowell's tactic had worked. Just then two deputies walked in.

"Stick around, Ed," said Brody. "I'm fixing to have a meeting with the boys. Give them some direction. We can continue our own little talk when I'm done with them."

Three more deputies walked in, and the five ambled over to stand in front of Brody's table. They looked nervously at each other. Finally, one of them spoke.

"Mr. Brody?" he said.

"Just hold your horses 'til the rest of you gets here," said Brody. "What I've got to say to you all I only want to say one time."

"Yes, sir," said the deputy.

The deputies shifted their weight from one leg to another, shuffled their feet, and looked at one another uneasily for another minute or two before the two stragglers finally showed up and joined them. Brody looked them over in silence, then he poured himself another brandy. He took a sip of the brandy, then a long pull on his cigar, blowing out the smoke in the general direction of his small army.

"While I was gone," he said solemnly, "on some very important business at the capitol, three of my deputies were brutally murdered. From what I hear, no one has come up with any evidence of any kind. So far, someone has gotten away clean with this awful crime. We can't allow that to happen. When I came to Drago, it was a lawless town. People were gunned down on the streets every day. Decent folks feared for their lives. I changed all that. I drove out the lawless elements and established a police force to maintain law and order. That's you men. And you ought to be as concerned about this as I am, even more concerned, because it was three of you that got killed. It might have been any three of you — any three of you standing there right now — as easy as it was Sneed and Bass and Olson. It could have been you, Harper, or you, Jones. Or any of the rest of you.

"And that's not the worst of it. The day after tomorrow is going to be the twenty-fifth anniversary of the founding of Drago, and we have a big celebration planned. Our town is going to be full of visitors, some of them important visitors. The eyes of the whole territory are at this moment fixed on Drago, on us, on you and on me. And what are they going to see? Murderers running loose in our town? Going unpunished? No, by God."

Here Brody bashed his fist down onto the table for emphasis, causing both bottles and both glasses to hop so that McDowell feared they would overturn. He clutched at the two bottles to steady them. Brody remained unconcerned about possible spillage.

"We are going to find that murderer and make him pay for his crime. I want him found by tomorrow night at the latest. I don't want that son of a bitch running loose once our celebration gets under way. In fact, I want to add his hanging to the official activities of the Twenty-fifth Anniversary Celebration of the Fine City of Drago."

Brody paused for dramatic effect and took another drink of brandy. He leaned back and looked over his captive audience. He looked each deputy in the face, individually, one by one.

"Is that perfectly clear?" he asked.

The deputies all muttered affirmative answers and nodded their heads.

"Then go on out there and get it done," said Brody.

"That was a fine and stirring speech, Phil," said McDowell. "If that doesn't motivate the men to get the job done, then nothing will. I hope you don't mind if I quote you in my reports of these events."

"Go right on ahead," said Brody. "Only one thing. Don't report none of this, not a single damned word, until we've got that bastard locked up in jail and waiting to hang. Then you write it up, and then you quote me."

It was late in the evening by the time Sheriff Phil Brody went home to the big blue house north of town. Susan was sitting on the divan with a glass of sherry in her hand. Her underthings were no longer scattered on the floor. When Brody came into the house, she did not bother rising to greet him.

"You've been back for hours," she said. That was all. The rest of the thought was clearly implied though. Brody tossed his hat at a hat tree that stood in a corner of the room. He missed, and it fell on the floor. He took off his gun belt and dropped it onto a small table. Then he strode over to his favorite chair, a large, overstuffed leather-covered thing with massive wooden armrests, and dropped heavily into it with a long, weary sigh.

"Get me a drink," he said.

Susan obeyed but without enthusiasm. She poured him a brandy and carried it to him. He took it from her and began to drink.

"Pick up my hat," he said, and she did. She hung it on the hat tree, then she went back to her seat on the divan and resumed sipping her sherry.

"A stranger came by here looking for you today," she said.

"What did he want?"

"He said he wanted a job. He had the look of a drifter to me, shiftless, no good. I wouldn't be surprised if he turns out to be some kind of a criminal. He had that look."

"Bullshit," said Brody. "What does a criminal look like, anyway? Did he have a name?"

"Robert D. Wade, I think," said Susan. "Yeah. Robert D. Wade. That was it. If I were you, if he comes around

64

again, I'd run him off. He has a dangerous look about him. I don't trust him. I don't like him."

"Yeah, well, you ain't me, and it ain't up to you. I don't think I need your advice about who to hire and who not to hire, or who to run off and who not to run off. Here. Get me another drink," said Brody. "While I was gone, someone killed three of my men. Three of my best men. It just happens that I'm shorthanded. I just might take a look at this . . . what did you say his name was?"

"Robert D. Wade."

"Yeah. I just might take a look at this Wade guy. Come here and pull my boots off."

Susan reached for the boot that Brody held up off the floor.

"Not like that," said Brody. "Turn around."

Susan knew what he wanted. She turned her back to him and straddled his leg, holding the boot by the heel in front of her in both hands. Brody put his other foot against her buttocks and shoved. The boot came off and Susan staggered forward a couple of steps.

"Now the other one," he said.

She repeated the process with the other leg, but this time, just as the boot started to come free of Brody's foot, he gave a hard shove with his other foot and sent Susan sprawling face forward on the floor. He threw back his head and laughed heartily at his joke. Susan, lying on the floor, flushed with anger. She knew that it would only make things worse to give voice to her anger, so she kept quiet. Let him have his laugh. She stood up and took his boots to a corner of the room. Yes, she thought, let him have his laugh. I'll have mine later, and I'll have mine last. I'll get my way. He will hire Robert D. Wade just because I told him not to, and Robert D. will kill Phil Brody for me. He'll do it for me.

"You've got four other men coming in already," she said. "You don't need this one."

"Three was just killed," said Brody. "Don't you hear good? That means I'll only be one ahead of where I was when those four get here. I was planning on increasing my force by four. So I got four coming, but I lost three. Any way you look at it, I'm coming up short. Robert E. Wade, huh?"

"D."

"What?"

"Robert *D*. Wade," Susan repeated, emphasizing the middle initial.

"Whatever," said Brody, and he took another sip of brandy.

Chapter 8

Robert D. and his companions went into the Tangle-foot. They noticed that they were getting some hard looks from around the room, and a couple of the people staring at them were uniformed deputies.

"Let's get a table," said Robert D.

He spotted an available one and led the way to it. Trish pulled out a chair and sat down.

"I'll get us a bottle," said Robert D. "Be right back."

He headed for the bar, and Pawnee sat down across the table from Trish.

"We're getting some pretty mean stares," said Trish. "Have you noticed?"

"Yeah," said the scout. "I noticed."

"How come?"

"For one thing," said Pawnee, "not many girls sit in bars. They're wondering about you."

"For one thing?" she said. "What's the other?"

Robert D. came back to the table with a bottle and three glasses. He pulled out a chair and sat down between the other two. He poured three glasses of whiskey, pushing one toward Trish and another toward Pawnee.

"There you go," he said.

Pawnee picked up his glass and downed it in a gulp. He shoved the empty glass back toward Robert D.

"It didn't hold much," he said.

Robert D. refilled it. Trish had sipped at hers, and Robert D. hadn't yet lifted his own glass off the table.

"Pawnee," said Trish.

"Yeah?"

"What's the other?"

"The other what?" asked Robert D.

"Pawnee was telling me why people are staring at us in here. He said for one thing I'm a girl. Okay. I'm waiting for the other thing. What is it?"

"Me," said Pawnee.

"What about you?" said Trish. "Why would they be staring at you?"

"If we stay in here long enough, you'll see."

Trish looked at Robert D., puzzled, but all he did was shrug and take a drink of whiskey. She sipped at her own drink, trying to ignore the stares. Looking over her glass, she caught the eye of a bulky frontier type at a nearby table. The man looked particularly surly. For an instant, Trish thought that he was staring at her, but then she realized that he was, indeed, directing his glare at Pawnee. Others around the room looked away when she glanced at them, but this man kept staring.

"Robert D.," said Trish, "I don't like this. Let's get out of here."

Pawnee tossed down his second drink and stood up.

"Come on," he said. "I'll walk you back to your room."

Robert D. nodded and poured himself another drink. Trish gave him an uncertain look, hesitated for an instant, then stood up and headed for the door. Pawnee was right beside her. The bulky man at the nearby table watched as they left the saloon. Robert D. took note of the man and smiled to himself as he sipped his whiskey.

Outside, Trish and Pawnee walked along the wooden sidewalk headed for the hotel. Trish waited until they were about halfway there before she spoke.

"Pawnee," she said, "why was that man staring so hard at you?"

"Aw," said Pawnee, "it ain't much. I put up with it all

my life, everywhere I go. Some folks just seem to think that I show my Indian too much, that's all."

Trish stopped and stared at Pawnee incredulously.

"Well, to hell with them," she said.

"That's what I always say," said the scout. "Come on."

They walked on to the hotel and went upstairs. Pawnee waited while Trish unlocked the door to her room. He longed to follow her in, to put his arms around her and give her comfort. He longed for more than that. He wanted to tell her just how he felt about her, but he knew that he could never do that. He would just have to live with his secret, the secret that he kept from even his two friends. He watched her step into the room.

"Lock the door," he said.

"I will," said Trish. "And don't you go out and get yourself into any trouble. You hear me?"

"Aw, you know me."

"Yeah," she said. "That's why I said that."

Pawnee smiled and touched the brim of his hat.

"Good night," he said.

Back in the Tanglefoot, Robert D. noticed the big man get up and leave his table. The big man gave Robert D. a sideways look as he passed him by on his way to the door. The man had waited long enough, thought Robert D., so that his exit following Pawnee and Trish would not appear to be suspicious to anyone, especially to him. But the man was alone, and by the time he got outside, Pawnee would be on his way back from the hotel, also alone. With Trish safe in her room, Robert D. wasn't worried. Pawnee could take care of himself. The big man would be sorry if he tried anything with the scout. Robert D. poured himself another drink and took a sip.

Pawnee saw the big man lounging beside the door to

the Tanglefoot, and he felt almost certain that the man was waiting for his return. He knew the type. As he had just told Trish, he had dealt with them all his life. He stopped for a moment and looked toward the man. Then he heaved a sigh and moved on. Pawnee was not a man to look for a fight, but he would not be intimidated, either. He walked on to the Tanglefoot, and as if he had not noticed the big man, he started to walk through the swinging doors. The big man was surprisingly quick. He stepped in front of Pawnee and put a hand on the scout's chest, shoving him back.

"I thought maybe you got smart when you left a while ago," he said. "I guess I was wrong."

"What's your problem, friend?" asked Pawnee.

The big man snorted a half laugh. "I guess maybe I am your friend," he said. " 'Cause I'm just about to give you some real friendly advice."

"I'm listening," said Pawnee.

"Don't try to go back in there."

"And just why shouldn't I?"

"Well, now," said the big man, "I suppose I could be wrong. It could just be them clothes you're wearing. It's kind of hard to be sure, so you tell me."

"What do you want to know?"

"Just what are you?"

Pawnee looked the big man straight in the eyes. "I'm a human being," he said. "Male. I'm a man, the same as you."

"What kind?" asked the big man.

"I'm an American," said Pawnee. "Ain't you?"

"That ain't what I mean," said the big man, his voice betraying frustration and impatience. "What kind of American are you?"

"Is there more than one kind?" asked Pawnee.

"Damn it, give me a straight answer. Are you a goddamned Indian?"

"Oh," said Pawnee. "I see what you're getting at. Well, sir, I'm half white."

"What's the other half?"

"Pawnee Indian."

"By God, I thought so. Well, Indians ain't allowed in saloons here, so you just turn around and walk away, and we won't have no more trouble."

"I didn't know we'd had any trouble," said Pawnee. "Excuse me."

"You ain't going back in there," said the big man.

"Why not?"

"I just told you, damn it. Indians ain't allowed."

"And I just told you," said Pawnee. "I'm half white. Are white men allowed?"

"Sure, but—"

"Then how can you keep my white half out of there? Seems to me like that would be illegal."

"But you ain't all white."

"I ain't all Indian, either."

"Damn it, I'm through arguing with you," said the big man. "You ain't going in."

Pawnee sighed in resignation and looked down at the sidewalk.

"Well," he said, "I guess we're bound to have a fight." He held out his right hand toward the big man.

"My name's Pawnee O'Rourke," he said. "What's yours?"

"What?"

"What's your name? I can't fight a man I never even met."

"Alfie Dolan," said the big man.

Pawnee stood still for a moment, his right hand extended. Alfie Dolan just stood there giving Pawnee a stupid look.

"Well?" said Pawnee.

"What?" said Dolan.

"Well, shake hands so we can get this fight started and get it over with."

Dolan, the stupid expression lingering on his face, shook Pawnee's hand.

"You want to step out in the street?" questioned Pawnee.

Dolan followed Pawnee out into the street, and the two men squared off for a fight.

"Fight," someone yelled from the door of the Tanglefoot, and soon men were pushing their way through the door to get outside to watch. From his place inside, Robert D. noticed that the men who had been sitting with Dolan had gotten up.

"Hell," he said. He picked up his bottle and his glass and went outside to keep an eye on them. Pawnee could handle the big man, but Robert D. thought that he might have to make sure the man's friends didn't decide to get in on the action. He located them in the crowd outside and watched.

Pawnee and Dolan were circling each other. The crowd was yelling for someone to start swinging. Finally, Dolan telegraphed a roundhouse right aimed at Pawnee's head. Pawnee stepped aside and easily avoided the blow. Dolan staggered a bit from the force of his own swing. He recovered his balance and took aim for a second punch. Again he telegraphed, again Pawnee sidestepped, and again Dolan staggered.

"Come on, Alfie," someone shouted.

"Stand still and fight," said Dolan.

"You mean stand still and let you hit me?" said Pawnee. "I ain't stupid."

Dolan swung again and Pawnee ducked, but this time, from his crouch, he sent forth a quick, hard left jab that dug into the big man's ribs.

"Uf," Dolan grunted.

Pawnee danced backward.

"Hit him, Alfie."

Dolan took a deep breath and rushed toward Pawnee. Pawnee stepped aside and jabbed Dolan on the ear as the big man rushed past him. Then Robert D. saw one of Dolan's drinking partners step out of the crowd. The man was right behind Pawnee and he reached around, grabbing the scout's arms and pinning them to his sides.

"Now hit him, Alfie," the man shouted.

Robert D.'s hand went to his Colt, but before he

could do anything with it, Dolan stepped up to Pawnee, reached over his shoulder, and grabbed the other man by the hair. He pulled him away from Pawnee and delivered a powerful right cross to the man's jaw. The man fell back like a log and didn't move again. Dolan looked around at the crowd.

"Stay out of this," he said. "This is my fight."

Robert D. released his grip on his Colt. Pawnee didn't need his help. He had the help of the big man who was trying to beat him to a pulp.

"Thanks, Alfie," said Pawnee.

"You're welcome," said Dolan. "Now let's fight."

They circled each other again, and then, as Dolan made another attempt at a roundhouse, Pawnee stepped in under the man's long arm and, ducking his head, pounded a series of short, quick, hard jabs into the big man's midsection. Dolan flailed uselessly with his arms for a bit, then clutched with them, but before he had clamped down, Pawnee twisted and grabbed some shirt. He flung Dolan over his head, and the big man landed on his back with a dull thud. He lay there still for a moment, all the air knocked from his lungs, and he gasped for breath. Pawnee watched and waited.

"Why ain't he kicking him?" someone asked.

Finally, Dolan rolled over onto his stomach, then got up to his hands and knees. He stayed like that for a while, still sucking in deep breaths, then he straightened up and got one foot on the ground.

"Are you all right, Alfie?" asked Pawnee.

"Hell, yes, I'm all right, and I'm coming at you again."

He lurched to his feet and raised his fists. Robert D. sighed and went back into the Tanglefoot to his table. He sat down and poured himself another drink. He had already seen this too many times. Unless he thought that Pawnee needed his help, he surely didn't need to watch. Back out in the street, Pawnee sidestepped several more of Dolan's telegraphed punches. Dolan was wearing himself out with his wild swings. They were powerful blows, and any one of them, had it landed, would have taken off Pawnee's head. Pawnee had landed a few blows, and he knew at this stage of the fight that it was almost useless to land more. It was nearly impossible to hurt the big man. He decided that he needed to do something to bring it to an end. Dolan swung another wild punch, and just as he was recovering his balance, Pawnee leapt into the air and kicked out with both feet, smashing them into the side of the big man's head. Dolan staggered back a few steps, then his knees buckled and he sank to the ground in a sitting position. Blood ran down the side of his head onto his shirt. He was dazed.

"It's over," he said. "Hell, I can't fight you. You don't fight right."

"It seems right enough to me," said Pawnee, "but I'm just as glad it's over. Here. I'll give you a hand up."

Dolan took the hand that Pawnee had extended, and the scout pulled the big man to his feet.

"Can I buy you a drink?" he asked.

"Huh," said Dolan. "You going in there?"

"Yeah."

"Well, hell, if I can't keep you out of there, I might as well drink with you."

"Come on," said Pawnee, and the two recent combatants walked arm in arm back into the Tanglefoot. Even Robert D. was surprised at this development, but he poured drinks all around and even called for a wet towel with which to mop the blood from Dolan's face.

Chapter 9

It was late that night when Robert D. and Pawnee left the hotel by the upstairs back door. They walked between the buildings back out to the main street. Robert D., in the lead, looked carefully out onto the street. No one was around. The two hurried down the street to Brody's office, where Robert D. quickly moved to the far side of the door and watched the north end of the street while Pawnee stopped short to watch the south end.

"It's okay," said Robert D.

"Clear this way," said Pawnee.

Robert D. bent over and shoved a folded piece of paper under the door. Then, straightening up, he said, "Let's go."

They retraced their steps and got back into the hotel without having been seen by anyone.

The following morning they went once again to Maude's for breakfast, and they selected a table just by the front window. By turning his chair slightly, Robert D. found that he commanded a good view of the sheriff's office. Robert D. was finished with his meal and drinking a third cup of coffee when he saw Brody unlock the door and go inside. He took a final sip of his coffee and stood up to leave.

"Pay for this, Pawnee," he said. "If you see Brody leave his office, watch where he goes. If he heads toward his house, fire off some shots. That should delay him and warn me. But don't get caught."

Across the street, Brody stepped inside the office and noticed the paper on the floor. He bent to pick it up, and he unfolded it as he walked across the room to his big desk. Sitting at the desk, he began to read.

Brody—
We got 7. We'll get the others. One at a time.
Then it'll be just you. You've had a death grip on this town long enough.

> The Avengers

Brody's face turned white. He rose to his feet in one quick motion. Clutching the paper, he rushed to the door, jerked it open, and practically ran out onto the sidewalk. He didn't bother closing the door to his office as he headed for the Tanglefoot. There would be at least two deputies there, maybe three. By the time he bashed his way through the swinging front doors of the Tanglefoot, Brody was in a sweat. He saw two deputies lounging at the bar.

"Harper," he shouted. "Jones. Get over here."

The two deputies turned, then moved quickly to meet their boss. Brody thrust the letter at them.

"Read this," he said. Harper took it and began reading. Jones leaned over to read it at the same time.

"Who done this?" asked Jones.

"Who done it?" said Brody. "You see a name on the damn thing? How do I know who done it?"

"Well, where'd it come from, boss?" asked Harper.

"It was under my office door when I opened up this morning. Just now. Some sneaking coward must have slipped it under there last night sometime. It's some of these sneaking, cowardly bastards in town. They're too damn scared of me to face me in the open, so they're doing this. Get out there and find out who's behind this. Get going."

Harper and Jones headed for the door.

"Wait," shouted Brody. "Wait a minute. Just one of you go. Harper, you go gather up the others. Gather them up over at my house, so you can tell everybody without pulling the guards away from my house. Tell them again—all but them two guards—tell them to get out and find out who the hell is doing these things. Now go on. Jones, you stay here with me."

As Harper raced out the door, Brody headed for his special reserved table, and even though it was a little early, even for the sheriff, Burl came running with the special brandy and a glass.

"Seven," said Brody out loud to himself. "What seven?"

Across the street, Pawnee and Trish were watching.

"What do we do?" asked Pawnee. "Brody ain't headed for his house, but that deputy is."

"We follow him," said Trish. "No. Wait. I'll follow him. You keep an eye on Brody."

"Be careful," said Pawnee.

At the blue house, Robert D. was engaged in a deep and passionate embrace with Susan Brody. Finally, he tore himself loose.

"Your husband might come home," he said.

"He never comes home during the day," said Susan. "He can't stand my company. It's all right."

She pulled Robert D. close to her again, and her parted lips met his in a feverish, desperate kiss. Robert D. knew that he should leave, but she was very lovely, very inviting, and she had a way of making him believe for a while that none of the troubles, none of the problems, none of the ugly realities outside really existed.

Outside the Brody home but hanging back at some distance, Trish watched Harper head for the house. Her hand went to the six-shooter at her side. Then Harper's path veered slightly, and it became obvious to Trish that he was headed for the backyard and not for the house. She breathed a sigh of relief and allowed her hand to relax and fall away from the pistol. She would watch to make sure the deputies stayed in the backyard. Harper spoke to the two guards for a brief time, then he left again. Trish decided to stay and watch the house. Robert D. was in there with that woman. Pawnee would keep watch on Brody. She stayed. Soon two more deputies showed up. They went into the backyard. Something was going on. Trish counted as more deputies arrived at the house. When Harper came back with two more deputies, eight of them had gathered there behind the blue house. Eight. Where was the other one? Of course, she recalled, he was back at the saloon with Brody. Brody, the back-shooting coward. Brody had read the note and was afraid to be alone, unprotected. She saw the granite spire there in the yard where the deputies were meeting, and she thought for a moment about going back to the Tanglefoot. There would be only Brody and one deputy. She and Pawnee could take them easy. But what about Bobby? Would she be able to get Bobby out of the ground to take him home? Would the other deputies continue to guard the house and defend the town after Brody was dead? She didn't know. But if they did, the rest of her job would be more difficult. She would have revealed herself and her partners as the mysterious Avengers. Besides, she realized, she couldn't go away and leave Robert D. alone in the house with eight men out back. Something might go wrong there. She would stay for the time being. She would wait.

* * *

Robert D. stood up to pull on his trousers. As he fastened them at the waist, Susan threw her arms around him once more. She kissed him again.

"Robert D.," she said into his ear, "I love you. I love you. Come back to me soon. How much longer will it be?"

"I hope it won't be long, babe," said Robert D., freeing himself from her embrace. He pulled on his boots, then he put his shirt on. "Oh, yeah," he said, finding a piece of paper in the shirt pocket. "I need you to do something with this."

"What is it?"

"It's just part of the plan," said Robert D. "After I'm gone, make ol' General bark. Wait a couple of minutes, then take this to those guys out back. Say someone slipped up on the porch and stuck this under the front door. Say that's why the dog barked. Say you went to look and found this, but the scoundrel had already run away. You got all that?"

"Yes," said Susan, taking the paper. "I've got it, you scoundrel."

When Robert D. joined Trish outside where she waited, still some distance away, he heard the dog bark back at the house. He looked over his shoulder and smiled.

"I think I got out clean," he said. "Did you see anyone who might have spotted me?"

"No," said Trish. "We're safe."

"By the way, girl, what are you doing here? You were supposed to watch Brody unless he headed this way."

"Pawnee stayed with Brody," she explained. "One of the deputies headed this way, so I followed him. The whole bunch gathered up behind the house and had a real serious powwow for a while . . . all but one, who stayed with Brody in the Tanglefoot. Then they all headed out again, except those two guards back there."

"I think we've got him good and scared," said Robert

D. "Watch this now."

They were standing beside the last building in Drago to the north. There was nothing but space between them and the blue house. Robert D. pulled Trish around the corner of the building so that they were standing on the board sidewalk and facing the street. Still they watched the blue house out of the corners of their eyes. Susan went screaming into the backyard. She's good, Robert D. thought. She puts on a good act. A hell of a good act. The two deputies rushed to her aid. The distance was too great for Robert D. and Trish to make out what was being said, but they could tell that the voices were frantic, and they could see that Susan was waving a piece of paper before the deputies' faces. The deputies held a quick conference, then one of them left the yard and headed toward town. Robert D. and Trish looked at each other and smiled. They turned and began walking back toward Maude's, where they had abandoned Pawnee. When they had picked up the scout, Robert D. kept walking. The other two followed him.

"Where we going now?" asked Trish.

"I thought we'd get our horses and ride out to visit the Van Tuyls," said Robert D. "That okay with you?"

As the deputy ran into the Tanglefoot, Brody jumped to his feet.

"Hiram," he roared, "what the hell are you doing here? You're supposed to be guarding my house, ain't you?"

"Yes, sir," said Hiram Sand, "but someone left this here note at your house. I thought you'd want to know about it right away."

"Jones, go down there and take his place," said Brody, his voice suddenly quiet. He held out his hand toward Sand. Jones left the saloon as Sand handed the note to Brody. The sheriff turned the paper around and held it up before his eyes. His hand was trembling.

Brody—
You're a dead man. You just don't know it yet.

The Avengers

Lisa Van Tuyl welcomed them like old friends. They gathered again around the table, and Lisa poured them each a cup of coffee.

"What can we do?" asked Dutch. "I know, with what all you're up against, this ain't just a social visit."

"If you was to go into the Tanglefoot this evening, Dutch," said Robert D., "would there likely be anyone there you could get yourself into a casual conversation with without arousing no suspicion?"

"Well, sure," said Dutch. "A lot of my customers hang out there. I imagine I'd run into somebody. I don't go in there myself. Hardly ever. But, yeah, I know some who do."

"Good," said Robert D. "I got some things I'd like you to say where ol' Brody might just happen to overhear."

Edgar Wilhelm McDowell was walking down the sidewalk when one of Brody's deputies almost ran into him.

"Whoa there, boy," said McDowell. "Where's the fire?"

"Ain't no fire, Mr. McDowell," said the deputy. "Somebody's sending death threats to Sheriff Brody. We got to try to find out who it is who's doing it."

"Is the sheriff in his office?" asked McDowell.

"No, sir. He's down at the Tanglefoot."

As the deputy raced on, McDowell headed for the Tanglefoot. Brody had told him not to write anything just yet, but he was still a newspaperman. Here were some new developments. He walked on down the street and went into the saloon.

"Ed," shouted Brody when he spotted McDowell,

81

"come on over here and sit down. Have a drink. Hey, Burl. Get Mr. McDowell a drink."

"It's a little early for me," said McDowell. "Bring me some coffee."

"Yes, sir," said Burl.

"What's this about death threats, Phil?" asked McDowell.

"Goddamn it," said Brody. "Who's been blabbing?"

"Now, calm down. I just ran into Earl Collins out on the street. That's all. Nobody's blabbing around town."

"Well, it's true," said Brody. "When I opened up my office this morning, I found this. Slipped under the door."

He handed the offending note to McDowell, who read it with obvious interest. Then Brody handed over the second note.

"And some brazen bastard just a little while ago in broad daylight stuck this one under the front door of my house. Walked right up onto my porch and just stuck it under there. Right under the door. General barking. My wife in the house. Deputies out in the backward. And no one saw the son of a bitch. No one."

"The Avengers," mused McDowell. He was seemingly quite taken with the drama, with the romance of it all. "I wonder if they ride by night with sacks over their heads."

"Damn it," roared Brody. "It ain't funny."

"No," said McDowell. "Of course not. Don't worry so much, Phil. You'll get them. You got Bobby Madison and his gang, didn't you? And, besides, you're very well protected."

"I don't even know who they are," said Brody. "And I'm shorthanded. You seem to forget. I lost three men . . . maybe seven. I ain't figured that out yet. Everyone's accounted for. The only thing I can think of is if they got them four that was supposed to be coming here. They ain't showed yet, and they should have by now. That must be it. They got them four somehow. And this is who done it. These damned Avengers, whoever in hell they are.

"Ed, have you ever heard of a man named Robert D. Wade?"

"No, I don't believe so. Why?"

"He came to my house to ask for a job. I wasn't home. It was while I was still at the capitol. He told Susan. She told me not to hire him. She didn't like his looks. Said he was too mean-looking."

McDowell took a sip of his coffee while Brody poured himself another brandy.

"You think he might be behind this Avenger stuff?" asked McDowell.

"No. Hell, no," scoffed Brody. "These so-called Avengers is someone from right here in Drago. They got to be. Nothing else makes any sense. No. I'm thinking that if this Wade is half as tough as Susan thinks he is, that I might ought to give him a job. I'm short three men—or seven, depending on how you look at it. I need someone. I ain't seen him yet, and there's so damn many strangers in town getting ready for the Celebration that I can't even figure out who he might be. If you run across him, send him to see me."

"I'll do that, Phil," said McDowell. "In the meantime, I'll check the newspaper files to see if I have any information on him. Robert D. Wade, you say?"

"That's the man's name," said Brody. "Robert D. Wade."

Chapter 10

Pawnee kept watch for Robert D. that evening at the front window in the upstairs hallway of the hotel until he saw Dutch Van Tuyl park his wagon down on the street, secure it, and walk into the Tanglefoot. Robert D. gave it another twenty minutes, then he made his way over here. Walking into the saloon, he went straight to the bar. He didn't look at anyone, didn't acknowledge that he knew anyone, and he ordered a shot of Bourbon County whiskey. He had noted out of the corner of his eye, however, that Dutch Van Tuyl was seated at a table with three other men, just next to that of Brody. The sheriff, too, was there at his special table. He, too, had company. Seated next to Brody was a dignified white-haired gentleman in a gray business suit. Robert D. had not seen the man before.

"Look," said Dutch in a loud whisper to his drinking companions. "Looky there. Well, I'll be."

"What?" said one of the men at the table.

"Over there at the bar. He just walked in."

"Who you talking about, Dutch? That stranger? Just come in? Rough-looking fellow?"

"Yeah. Don't you know who that is?"

"Never seen him before."

"Phil, I think that—" McDowell began, but he was cut off abruptly by Brody.

"Shh. Wait a minute."

Brody's paranoid mind was preoccupied with all the strangers in Drago, and he was straining to eavesdrop on the conversation at the next table.

"That's Robert D. Wade," said Dutch. "Himself. In person."

"Robert D. Wade? Never heard of him."

But Sheriff Brody had, and he was listening even more intently. He leaned slightly in the direction of the table at which Dutch and his companions sat, and his eyes were fixed on Robert D.'s back.

"Robert D. Wade," said Dutch, his voice still a harsh whisper. "I can't believe you said that. Never heard of Robert D. Wade? Hell, man, I think he's wanted in five or six states. He's not wanted here, as far as I know. Probably why he's here."

"What's he wanted for?"

"Killings mostly," said Dutch. "He's a gunfighter. Why, five or six years ago, back in Missouri—Springfield it was—I saw him—Robert D. Wade—kill three men right down on the town square in the middle of the day, and they were all shooting at him. I mean, it was a fair fight. Got them all clean. And he didn't get a scratch. I never saw anything like it. Never hope to again. That's him. Right there."

Brody didn't want to react too quickly. He turned his attention back to McDowell.

"Now, Ed," he said, "what was it you was going to say?"

He allowed McDowell to talk for a few minutes, but he wasn't really listening. Soon Dutch got up and bade his companions good night. He'd catch hell at home if he stayed out too late or got too drunk, he said. They laughed and called him a few appropriate names, and he left the saloon. Only then did Brody move. He motioned McDowell to move over close to him. Then he spoke in a low, confidential voice.

"Did you find out anything on Wade?" he asked.

"I couldn't find a thing," said McDowell.

"Well, that's him right over there."

McDowell followed Brody's gaze to Robert D.'s back.

"He looks like a hardcase," said McDowell.

"Yeah," said Brody. "Go over there and ask him to join us for a drink. On me."

"All right."

McDowell got up and walked to the bar. He nudged his way in to stand next to Robert D., just to his left.

"Excuse me, sir," he said.

Robert D. ignored him.

"Mr. Wade?"

"You talking to me?" asked Robert D., turning his head only slightly toward McDowell.

"Yes, sir. You are Robert D. Wade?"

"Who wants to know?"

"I'm Edgar Wilhelm McDowell. I'm the local newspaper publisher and editor."

"You're the fellow that wrote that book they're hawking around town, too, ain't you?" said Robert D.

"Ah, yes, I have written a book that's on sale locally. You are Mr. Wade?"

"Yeah. You looking for someone else to write about?"

"Well," said McDowell, "that's not a bad idea. Maybe later. Right now I came over here to invite you to sit down with Sheriff Brody and myself. Sheriff Brody would like to buy you a drink. That's Sheriff Phil Brody."

"The man who killed Bobby Madison," added Robert D.

"Yes. He is the subject of my book. Have you read it?"

"I picked up a copy."

"Will you join us for a drink?"

"First time a sheriff ever offered to buy me a drink," said Robert D. "What's it all about?"

"I'm afraid you'll have to ask Sheriff Brody," said McDowell.

Robert D. followed McDowell over to Brody's table, and the sheriff made a wild and demanding gesture toward Burl, who responded instantly. When Robert D. arrived at the table, Brody stood up and offered his hand. Robert D. pretended not to notice. He pulled out a chair and sat down.

"Bourbon County whiskey," he said.

Burl hustled off to the bar.

"This man says you want to talk to me," said Robert D.

"That's right," said Brody.

"What about?"

"Well," said Brody, "I understand that you dropped by my house to see me. Something about a job."

"Oh, yeah," said Robert D. Just then Burl reappeared, and Robert D. stopped talking. He waited for the bartender to conclude his business and leave. Then he resumed. "I thought it over since then."

"You change your mind?" asked Brody.

"Let's just say I ain't sure."

"Why not? What's the problem?"

"I ain't never wore no badge," said Robert D. "And I sure don't want to wear no funny uniform. I took off my uniform at the end of the war. Swore I'd never wear another one."

"We might be able to work something out," said Brody. "You could work sort of undercover. You know? I need someone like you, Wade. I had twelve deputies to keep order in this town. Someone just killed three of them. There were four more coming and they ain't showed. I'm afraid the same killer got to them. I'm shorthanded, and we ain't got no idea who the killer is. I'll pay you top wages. You answer to me, no one else."

"How do you know I didn't kill them three?" asked Robert D.

Brody leaned back in his chair and laughed.

"Why?" he said. "I don't even know you. You're a stranger here. Why would you come to Drago and kill three of my men?"

"I might have been trying to create a job opening," said Robert D.

"No," said Brody. "Hell, I know who's behind it. I mean, I don't know exactly, but I know that it's someone local, someone who resents my control of the town. I've got two threatening letters just today. They're both signed the same way. The Avengers. Come on, Wade. What do you say? We've got a big celebration starting here in the morning. Lots of outsiders coming to town. Hell, there's a lot of them here already. On top of that, we got these killers running loose and making threats on my life. It ain't no time for me to be caught short. What do you say?"

"You said you lost three men," said Robert D. "Maybe seven."

"That's right."

"And you want me to take their place? Just one man?"

"You're all that I see around and available," said Brody.

"I've got a partner. Name of Pawnee O'Rourke. Me and him rode in together, along with my niece. Pawnee's a good man. He's better than any other three men all by himself."

"Funny," said Brody. "That's just what I heard about you."

"So you'd be getting six for the price of two. That's the only way I'll take it. Me and Pawnee and no damned uniforms."

"You got a deal, Wade," said Brody, and he stuck his hand across the table toward Robert D. This time Robert D. took it. The deal was made. "I need to meet O'Rourke."

"He'll probably be in here directly," said Robert D.

Edgar Wilhelm McDowell went back to his office that

night. To hell with Brody, he thought. I made Brody. The story was just too good to sit on. Phil Brody, the man who killed Bobby Madison who had killed Kid Conley, had just received two death threats, each one signed by The Avengers. The big celebration for Drago's twenty-fifth birthday was coming up in the morning, and the Avengers, whoever they might be, after having killed three deputies, were still loose. Then Robert D. Wade had showed up in town, another notorious gunman. McDowell saw in Wade a gold mine. With Brody, he had needed to create a character. Yes, Brody had killed Madison, but he had probably not done so in a fair fight. McDowell had not seen the actual killing, but he knew that the circumstances had been rather mysterious. Brody had probably murdered the man. But this Wade. He was a genuine frontier character. Writing about Wade wouldn't even take much creative energy. The character was already there, and he was real. McDowell sat down at his desk and began to write. He would roust Mel, his printer, out of the sack in a little while. The celebration would be under way in the morning, and this story needed to be on the front page.

It was late when McDowell finished his story and had set the grumbling typesetter-printer unexpectedly back to work. He strolled happily over to the Tanglefoot, where he found Brody still sitting at his reserved table with Robert D. He rejoined them, a smug, satisfied expression, on his face, but he made no mention of where he had been or what he had just done. He had just poured himself a drink when Pawnee and Trish walked in. Robert D. waved them over to Brody's table.

"Brody," he said, "this here is my partner, Pawnee O'Rourke. And that's my niece Trish with him. Y'all sit down. Pawnee, this is our new boss, Sheriff Phil Brody."

Trish felt her whole body stiffen, but she fought the feeling and sat down with a smile.

"I'm pleased to meet you, Sheriff Brody," she said. "I've heard a lot about you."

"Please," said Brody, "call me Phil. The pleasure is all mine."

His leer was not very well hidden. Others in the saloon were staring at Trish. They might have been staring because she was a beautiful young woman, or because she was a young woman dressed in men's clothing and sporting a gun. They might also have been staring at her because ordinarily the only women in the Tanglefoot were the whores who worked there for Brody. Some of them probably remembered her from the night of Pawnee's fight with Alfie Dolan. Brody forced himself to look away from Trish to acknowledge Pawnee.

"O'Rourke," he said, "I'm glad to have you with me. I'm not ashamed to tell you two that I'm a whole lot relieved. You're both on the payroll as of right now, and I want you to stay here until the place closes up tonight or until I decide to go on home. Whichever comes first. I'll let you know."

Brody kept pouring down the brandy until Burl had to bring him a second bottle. At one point, he had to excuse himself to go out back, and he made a uniformed deputy accompany him on that trip. Robert D. looked at McDowell.

"Does he always drink like this?" he asked.

"Sheriff Brody's a hard drinker," said the journalist, "but I've never thought of him as a drunk. I've never seen him this bad before. I think—" McDowell paused, considering his investment in Brody, weighing it against the commercial possibilities he saw in Robert D. Wade, "I think he's scared of these so-called Avengers. That's not to be repeated, of course."

"I don't give a damn one way or the other," said Robert D., "except that we just took a job from the man."

When Brody came back in, he staggered over to the table but did not take his customary seat. He dropped

90

heavily and clumsily into the empty chair that was right next to Trish. Then he spoke to Robert D., but his eyes were on the girl.

"You have a beautiful niece here, Wade," he said. "Yes, indeed."

Trish felt revulsion well up from deep in the pit of her stomach. She repressed it and smiled.

"Thank you, Mr. Brody," she said.

Brody reached an arm around the back of Trish's chair and leaned over close to her. She smelled his foul, drunken breath.

"Would you like to see the rest of my facility here?" he asked her. "There are some very nice rooms upstairs. I'd be happy to give you a tour."

Brody's voice was beginning to slur. His arm slipped off the back of the chair to encircle Trish's body from behind. He held her tight. His head almost rested on her shoulder, his face very close to hers. He gazed drunkenly into her eyes.

"Well," said Trish, "I—"

Pawnee's Remington .44 was out before anyone knew that he had made a move. It was held level and steady in an outstretched arm across the table, and it was aimed directly at Brody's face. Pawnee slowly thumbed back the hammer. He didn't speak. No one did for a long, tense moment. Brody stared at the barrel as if it had been a snake poised to strike. Across the room one of two uniformed deputies rose to his feet. His partner put a restraining hand on his shoulder, but he, too, stood up. Both deputies had their hands on the butts of their revolvers. They watched and waited. It was Robert D. who finally broke the silence.

"Brody," he said, "me and Pawnee here hired out our services to you. That don't include no services from Trish. You're drunk, man. Let us take you on home."

"No," said Brody. "Just take me upstairs. I'll just stay here tonight."

Robert D. got up and took hold of Brody. He helped

the drunken man to his feet.

"Come on," he said. Turning to Pawnee and Trish, he added, "I'll be right back."

Holding the weight of Brody on one side, Robert D. made his way to the stairs and climbed them. As soon as he and Brody disappeared at the top of the stairway, the two deputies made their move. Pawnee had just put away his Remington when he saw them coming at him. He reached for it again, but the deputies already had their weapons out. Both aimed for Pawnee, who threw himself and the chair in which he sat over to his left, pulling his right-side Remington at the same time. Two slugs smashed into the floor just behind where Pawnee had been. The scout came up to his knees and fired across the table, his bullet tearing into the chest of one deputy. The other had just drawn a bead on Pawnee, when Trish, who had kicked over her chair and come to her feet, fired her own six-gun. The man staggered back, clutching at his guts. She fired again, smashing his sternum. His face went blank. His fingers relaxed, and his gun clattered to the floor. Then he sank to his knees and pitched over forward on his face.

Robert D. had just dropped Brody onto a bed upstairs when he heard the shots fired. Brody had passed out almost instantly upon landing on the mattress, so he knew nothing of what was going on, but Robert D. had his gun in his hand as he started back down the stairs. About halfway down he saw the two bodies, and he saw that Trish and Pawnee were all right. He also saw McDowell just emerging from the cowering position he had taken almost under the table. He slowed his pace and came on down the stairs. Walking over to the table, he asked, "What happened here?"

McDowell recovered quickly once the danger was past, and it was he who responded to Robert D.'s question.

"Just a misunderstanding," he said. "Unfortunate. These two wretches here on the floor thought that you two were a threat to Sheriff Brody. Understandable, since they had seen Mr. O'Rourke's pistol aimed at the sheriff, and they were too far away to hear anything that had been said. Their mistake was that they came too fast with their guns out. They should have asked questions first. My God, I've never seen anything like it. Excuse me. I've got to get back to my office."

Back at the newspaper office, McDowell yelled to his sleepy-eyed printer.

"Don't run that off yet," he said. "I've got to add the latest episode."

Chapter 11

The big celebration wasn't really scheduled to begin until noon, the first official items on the agenda being speeches to be followed by fireworks and a big free barbecue, but the people were already in town. They had come by the droves, and nothing would hold them back. The sun had barely made its appearance when the first fireworks were set off. Random gunshots were soon added to the general clamor, some of them were fired into the air by unruly young men racing down the main street on horseback. Following a breakfast at Maude's, Robert D., Pawnee, and Trish had gone back to the Tanglefoot. Ordinarily, it wouldn't have been open so early, but the hours had been extended for the festivities. Some people would start early and drink all day. Besides, the new deputies were supposed to be protecting Brody, and the sheriff was still sleeping off a drunk upstairs in the Tanglefoot. They seated themselves at Brody's reserved table and ordered coffee from Burl.

The uniformed deputies Jones and Harper came in to stand their Tanglefoot guard duty. Hogan and Sand were on duty at the blue house, and the two remaining deputies were patrolling the streets. Jones had a copy of the morning paper, and he and Harper eyed Robert D. and his companions suspiciously. Another copy of the morning paper lay on the bar. Back at Brody's table, Trish leaned toward Robert D. to speak confidentially.

"Uncle Bob," she said, "what are we waiting for? When do we make our move? I'm sick of looking at that bastard Brody and listening to him and just smiling. I don't know how much longer I can keep this up."

"We've already started," said Robert D. "We got five deputies. Five out of twelve, and that's not counting those four recruits. That ain't bad."

"That leaves seven," said Trish. "And Brody."

"And there's three of us," said Robert D. "That's not good odds for a frontal attack. We've been lucky so far. No one knows we got those first ones and those two last night made it easy. It looked like it was all their fault, a stupid mistake. Brody still don't know why we're here. He thinks we're on his side."

"He doesn't know what happened in here last night," said Trish. "He might change his mind when he finds out."

"We'll just have to wait and see."

"We could take those two over there right now," said Pawnee. "That would even up the odds just a little."

"We could," said Robert D. "but we ain't going to. Look, we all agree. We want to get Brody, and the only way to get Brody and to move Bobby is through his deputies. But I don't want us to do any deliberate murders, and I don't want us to take any fool chances. So you two just grin and bear it until I see the time is right. You got that?"

Pawnee shrugged, and Trish looked sulkily down at the tabletop in front of her. They might not like it, thought Robert D., but they would do as he said.

It was late morning when Brody began to revive. He

awoke with a dull, throbbing pain, which seemed to have settled itself just between and above his eyes and right on the inside of his skull. He groaned loudly and sat up on the edge of the bed, holding his head in his hands. It took him a couple of minutes to realize where he was. He tried to recall the events of the previous night, but the last thing he could remember was sitting at his table downstairs having a semi-pleasant conversation with his two new deputies — what were their names? Oh, yes. Robert D. Wade and Pawnee O'Rourke. Yes. He called them his special deputies because they would not be in uniform like the rest. Then Robert D.'s niece had joined them. A lovely young thing. Trish. He had no memory of anything beyond that, until waking up a moment ago with this pounding in his skull. The pain was almost unbearable, and when it reverberated following each beat down into and through his eyeballs, he wondered if it would eventually make him blind. He stood up on his feet unsteadily and started to make his cautious way downstairs.

"Don't look now," said Pawnee, "but here comes the boss, looking like something the dog dragged up to the back door."

Brody managed to make it to his table and sit down. Again he groaned. He acknowledged the presence of the three trespassers at his private table with a slight and very tenuous nod of his head.

"You look like you need a little hair of the dog," said Pawnee.

Brody made a noise that sounded like a possible agreement with that statement, so Pawnee made a wild gesture toward Burl.

"Burl, ol' buddy," he said, "bring Mr. B. here some of his favorite stuff."

Burl hurried over with the bottle and glass. Pawnee took it and poured the glass full, setting it down in front of Brody. The sheriff looked at it for a long moment, accusingly. Finally, he picked it carefully, lest his shaking hand cause its contents to slosh over the sides. He took an exploratory sip.

"How'd I get upstairs last night?" he asked.

"I hauled you up there," said Robert D.

Brody grunted. It might have been a thank you. Outside the fireworks and gunshots continued, and Brody winced a little with each bang.

"Celebration got started a little early," said Robert D.

"Yeah," groaned Brody, "I've got to make a goddamned speech here in a little while."

He finished his drink and reached for the bottle.

"One more ought to do the trick," he said.

At the bar, Burl's eye fell on the folded-up morning paper. He shot a glance at Brody, then swept the paper quickly back behind the bar. From across the room, Jones and Harper still stared with hard looks at the strangers at Brody's table. Finally, Jones spoke to Harper in a low voice.

"You reckon he's seen the story?" he asked.

"He ain't seen it," said Harper. "I can tell. He don't even know what happened."

"You reckon we ought to show it to him?"

"Yeah."

"He already looks to be in a pretty bad mood."

"So much the better," said Harper. "Let me have that damn newspaper. Come on."

Harper took the paper from the other deputy and led the way over to Brody's table, Jones following along none too sure of himself.

"Morning, boss," said Harper.

Brody looked up and grunted. "I don't suppose you've seen the morning paper?"

"No," said Brody, pouring himself another shot. "Just leave it on the table."

"There's a story on the front page I think you ought to read," said Harper. He opened the paper and laid it on the table before Brody, then stepped back and waited. Brody glanced at the paper. His eyes widened when he saw the headline: TWO MORE DEPUTIES KILLED IN DRAGO. He grabbed up the paper and started to read. His hands were still shaking so that the paper rattled as he held it up before his eyes and read the following story:

Last night, two more of Sheriff Phil Brody's team of crack deputies were killed in Drago. Unlike the previous three, however, these do not remain mysteries. The deputies, George Potter and Thomas Cole, were on duty at the Tanglefoot when they misinterpreted a gesture made by one Pawnee O'Rourke. Thinking that O'Rourke had threatened the life of the Sheriff, they came at him with six-guns drawn. O'Rourke was faster, and he was aided in the impromptu gun battle by a young and vivacious female shootist called Trish. Her last name has not yet been determined, but she came to Drago a few days ago in the company of O'Rourke and her uncle, the famous gunman Robert D. Wade. At the time of the shooting, Wade was upstairs in the Tanglefoot with Sheriff Brody. Neither Wade nor Brody was involved in the fracas.

The deputies killed previously, Warren Sneed, Buddy Bass, and Karl Olson, were found in the road north of Drago. So far neither their killers nor the reason for the killings has been determined. With the strength of Sheriff Brody's law enforcement team suddenly reduced from twelve to seven, our sheriff has sworn in both Wade and O'Rourke as special deputies. In the opinion of this writer, the young woman known as Trish would not be a bad choice for a third in that category.

All of this violence has come at a particularly embarrassing time for Sheriff Brody, the famous slayer of Bobby Madison, outlaw, and for the town of Drago, for it immediately preceded our Twenty-fifth Birthday Celebration, which gets underway officially this morning. We can take comfort, though, in the fact that our safety is being guarded by the likes of Robert D. Wade, Pawnee O'Rourke and the mysterious and beautiful Trish, not to mention our own Sheriff Phil Brody.

When Brody finished reading the story, he let the paper drop on the table there before him, and he stared ahead into space for a long, quiet moment. Finally, he poured himself another brandy and took a long sip. He set down the glass and looked at Trish, then at Pawnee.

"Is this true?" he asked.

"I ain't read it," said Pawnee.

Brody looked back at Trish. She shrugged and shook her head.

"Me neither," she said. "What's it say?"

"It says that you two killed two of my deputies in here last night. Right here. While I was upstairs with your uncle. You killed Potter and Cole. Is that true?"

"I don't know their names," said Pawnee. "We wasn't introduced, but we damn sure shot two fellows in here who was dressed in them cute little black suits."

"Why?" asked Brody.

"They didn't give us much choice," said Pawnee. "They come at us with guns ablazing."

"That's right," said Trish.

"Well," said Brody grudgingly, "that's what the paper says, but damn it, I hire you two to find out who killed three of my deputies and to protect me, and you just wind up killing two more of my men. Damn it to hell, ain't nothing going right lately."

Jones and Harper were beginning to feel conspicuous standing there by the table. The scene had not developed the way they had thought it would. They had expected Brody's wrath to center on the strangers, but it had not. He had apparently accepted the story as it had been printed, had accepted the strangers' version of the shooting. The uniformed deputies resented the special status of these newcomers with their boss, and they had hoped to cause them some problems. Their uneasiness was finally relieved when Brody spoke directly to Jones.

"Is that goddamned newspaperman over at his office?" he asked.

"He was just a little while ago," said Jones.

Brody heaved himself up out of his chair. He pointed a finger at Robert D.

"You all stay here," he said. His next words were for Jones and Harper as he walked past them, heading for the front door. "You two come along with me. This job don't call for no brains."

As Brody disappeared out the door with his two deputies, Trish looked at Robert D.

"I wonder what he's up to," she said. "I think I'll just tag along to see."

"Be careful, Trish," said Robert D.

"Don't worry."

Trish left the Tanglefoot and looked down the street in both directions. Her eyes found the three men she was looking for down close to the newspaper office. She stood there just outside the Tanglefoot and watched. They turned into the newspaper office, then she started to follow.

Edgar Wilhelm McDowell was sitting at his desk when Brody came bursting through the door to his office, followed by Harper and Jones. McDowell was startled by the sudden noise and the manner of Brody's intrusion. He tried to regain his composure.

"Good morning, Phil," he said with a forced smile on his face. "You feeling better this morning?"

McDowell knew that Brody was mad about the story. He had known when he made the decision to run it that Brody would be angered. The sheriff had told him not to write about the killings until the killer had been captured, but the story had just been too good, and McDowell had figured that he could convince Brody with smooth talk that it had all been in his best interests. He had always been able to manipulate the sheriff in that way before. He could do it again. Brody had not answered McDowell's inquiry regarding his disposition. Instead, he had stalked directly to a pile of copies of the morning edition of the paper. He picked one up and held it with the headline facing McDowell.

"What the hell is this?" he demanded.

"Phil," said McDowell, "sit down and let's have a talk. There's a good reason I ran that story, and I can explain . . ."

While McDowell had been speaking, Brody had been rolling the newspaper. He had rolled it into a bat, which he then used to give McDowell a vicious slap across the side of the face, knocking the journalist's wire-rimmed glasses askew. McDowell screamed more from astonishment and fright than from pain, although the blow did sting. He fumbled for his glasses, trying to straighten them, but Brody came across from the other side, dealing another hard slap.

"I told you not to run that story," said Brody, "didn't I?"

He slapped McDowell again and again. The newspaperman cringed in his chair, his arms up in front of his face, trying to ward off the blows. Finally, as suddenly as he had begun, Brody stopped. He flung the paper at

McDowell's head.

"Teach him a lesson, boys," he said to Jones and Harper, then turned his back on the scene and left the office. When Brody stepped outside, he did not turn back toward the Tanglefoot but in the other direction, heading for his own house. Trish watched him until she was sure of his destination, then she raced back to the saloon. Inside the newspaper office, Harper was turning over type cases. Jones took hold of McDowell's necktie and used it to pull the poor wretch to his feet. Then he smashed a fist into McDowell's midsection, knocking all the air out of his lungs. As McDowell gasped for breath, Jones dealt him a vicious right-hand blow to the side of his head. McDowell went sprawling to the floor in the midst of his scattered type. Harper stepped over to the editor's desk and, with a mighty heave, turned it over on its side. He spun around then, looking for something else to smash. Jones was kicking at McDowell's ribs and head.

Back at the Tanglefoot, Trish hurried over to Robert D. and Pawnee, where they still sat at Brody's table.

"What's up?" Robert D.

"They went to the newspaper office," she said. "They're smashing the place up and beating McDowell to a pulp. Brody headed on home and left the other two to do the dirty work."

Robert D. thought about the kind of parasite McDowell was and tried to weigh that against the brutal methods of Sheriff Phil Brody. He also considered the role he and Pawnee were playing with Brody. Trish stood fidgeting.

"Well?" she said.

"Oh, hell," said Robert D. "Let's go."

Chapter 12

By the time Robert D., Pawnee, and Trish arrived at the newspaper office, Harper and Jones were gone. They found McDowell on his hands and knees, trying hard to get to his feet. He was alone in the midst of a shambles that had once been his place of business. Robert D. sighed heavily. The man, he thought, had brought this all on himself with his scheme of trying to build a national hero from the likes of Phil Brody. He stepped over pieces of furniture and equipment to get to McDowell's side, then he reached down to help the man to his feet.

"Anything broken?" he asked.

"No, I don't think so," said McDowell. "My press. My office. He had no right."

"Well," said Robert D., "you can worry about that later. Right now, I think we better get you to a doc. Come on."

McDowell pushed Robert D. away from him.

"No," he said. "No. I'm all right. Just leave me alone. I'll be all right."

Robert D. looked back to where Trish and Pawnee stood by the door. Pawnee gave an unconcerned shrug.

"Go on," said McDowell. "Please."

Robert D. walked back to the door.

"Let's go," he said.

Alone once more, McDowell began to pick things up

from the floor.

He gathered up a handful of type and looked around for the tray, finally locating it on the floor, broken. He walked to a shelf that was attached firmly to the wall and was, therefore, one of the few items still in place, and he put the pieces of type up there. Then McDowell struggled to upright his desk. At last he got it in place, then he looked for the things that had been on top of the desk, picking them up one at a time and replacing them. Even if things were broken, he carefully put them back in their places. There had been a file cabinet standing in the corner back behind his desk and to his right when he was seated at his work. The drawers had been pulled out and thrown around the room and the cabinet overturned. He lifted up the cabinet and set it back in place. Then he found the top drawer and replaced it. Its contents were strewn all over the floor. It was when McDowell began picking them up and sorting through them that his gaze caught some of the papers from the Bobby Madison file. He searched for the folder they belonged in, found it, and replaced the papers, but the file was incomplete. He got down on his knees and hunted for the rest of the Bobby Madison papers. This was what had started the whole thing, he thought, the killing of Bobby Madison. When Brody had claimed credit for killing the famous outlaw, McDowell had dreamed up the exploitation of the event. He had gone to Brody and told him his plan, and the sheriff had gone for it like a tick for a dog's ear. And this was the thanks he got.

He found a few more papers and, thinking that the file was complete again, stood up with it, walked to his overturned chair, righted it, and replaced it behind the desk. Then he sat down with the Bobby Madison file. McDowell wasn't really looking for anything. He was simply musing morbidly, recalling all the events that had led up to this day, remembering the grand scheme he had contrived around the heroic figure of Sheriff Phil Brody. Then he saw the name. At first it didn't register. He looked again. There it was. Trish. He backed up. Bobby

Madison had a sister named Trish. It could be coincidence, he thought. He read on.

General set up a ferocious barking when he heard footsteps on the front porch of the blue house, and Susan hurried to the door to find out who was coming. Out on the porch, Brody fumbled furiously with the door handle. Finding the door locked, he began pounding on it and yelling.

"Open up the damn door," he shouted. "Shut up, General."

The dog recognized his master's voice and ceased his racket. Instead, he began running back and forth in the living room in anticipation of Brody's entrance. Susan unlocked and opened the door. Brody pushed her roughly aside as he entered the room. She closed the door and relocked it while General pawed at Brody, looking for attention.

"Go on," said Brody, kicking at the dog. "Put this goddamned dog in the other room."

"Come on, General," said Susan. "Come on."

She got the dog into another room and shut the door to keep him there. When she turned back, Brody was right behind her, almost touching her. She gasped in surprise, and he grinned.

"I scare you?" he asked.

His rancid odor filled her nostrils, and she thought that she would be sick if he didn't back off. He smelled of booze and sweat and she didn't know what else. It was a fetid, stale smell. She tried to slip around him to get out into the open space of the room, but he put his hands against the door behind her, one on either side of her head, and leaned forward to press his open mouth against hers. When he finally backed away from his slavering kiss, she turned her head to one side.

"You need a bath," she said. "You smell."

Brody slapped her hard on the side of her head, and Susan stifled a scream. Blood trickled out of a corner of her mouth.

"You don't talk to me like that," he said. He grabbed a handful of her hair and flung her around himself and down onto the floor. This time she did scream out loud. Before she could get to her feet, Brody had her by the hair again. He dragged her halfway up, then threw her against the wall. She fell to the floor, and Brody was on her. He rolled her over onto her back, then knelt astride her waist, sitting with his whole weight on her to hold her down. She reached up to fight against him, to defend herself against his attack. He grabbed her wrists, then held them both in his left hand. Still she struggled, and Brody slapped her face hard three times.

"Hold still, damn you," he said.

She ceased her struggles. Tears of pain and rage threatened to flow from her eyes. Susan wanted to scream and to cry, but she choked back the impulse. Brody reached down with his free right hand and ripped at the bodice of her dress until he had exposed both breasts. He clutched at first one, then the other, leaving finger marks behind, and then he dropped his head down and sucked and bit angrily.

"Phil, please don't," Susan finally managed to say. He stopped and stood up. Looking down at her, he began to unfasten his belt.

"Turn over," he said, "and get upon your knees."

The Tanglefoot was full of customers. Many of them were local people, but the majority were from out of town and had come for the big celebration. Burl and two other bartenders were busy keeping up with the orders for drinks. It was not only a large crowd, but it was also a loud one. Jones and Harper stood guard armed with shotguns. Outside it was even rowdier. Young cowboys still rode up and down the street at full gallop, yelling and firing their revolvers into the air. Young boys in bare feet were lighting firecrackers behind every building. Between the blue house and the town, carpenters were putting the finishing touches on the speaker's stand, and off to the side an army of cooks was sweating over a firepit in which several hundred pounds of beef sizzled. In the background, a small makeshift band was tuning its instruments. From between two buildings, a dog came running and howling, a string of lighted firecrackers tied to its tail. As it burst out onto the main street, it spooked a horse which then reared, dumping its half-drunk rider unceremoniously to the ground. A crowd of onlookers pointed and howled with laughter.

In the yard behind the blue house, a crowd hovered around the granite spire, having paid their ten cents each to view the grave of Bobby Madison. Some were leaving with rocks in their hands. Others crowded around the gate, waiting their turns. Hogan and Sand had all they could handle there. Two other deputies rode horses up and down the main street, watching the antics and letting the celebrants know it was all right to have fun, but there was a line that they had better not cross if they knew what was good for them. Robert D., Pawnee, and Trish had come out of the Tanglefoot to view all this wild activity. They stood beside the door, leaning against the wall. Down the street, unnoticed by anyone, Edgar Wilhelm McDowell walked out of his office and headed north. He was clutching a crumpled file folder to his breast. The expression on his face was intense.

When Brody backed away from his wife and stood up, his sadistic lust sated, Susan crawled to the nearest corner and pulled her knees up to her breasts. She glared at Brody. She would have killed him if she had thought she could.

"You bastard," she said, and she knew she was being a fool. If she antagonized him further, he would beat her more. "I hate your guts. I hope he does kill you."

Brody had been headed for his bedroom, but he stopped and turned back to face her.

"What did you say?" he demanded. "Who? Who are

you talking about?"

"I said I hate your guts," she said. "I called you a bastard."

She knew she had said too much, and she hoped that he would let it go by, but he didn't. He walked toward her menacingly, pausing only long enough to pick up the belt he had dropped on the floor earlier.

"You said more than that," he snarled. "You hope who kills me?"

"Whoever it is," she said. "Whoever killed those three out on the road. The Avengers. I don't care who does it."

"You say he," said Brody. "That sounds like you had someone special in mind. Who is he?"

"I told you. The Avengers."

Brody lashed at her with the belt. "The Avengers is *they*," he said. "You said *he*. Who is he?"

He lashed at her again. Susan screamed and pressed herself into the corner.

"Tell me," said Brody, and he lashed again.

"Robert D.," she screamed. "Robert D. Wade. God. Stop it."

Brody stood, the belt dangling from his right hand. He looked at her in disbelief.

"You're lying," he said.

"No, I'm not," said Susan. "He came here to kill you."

"How do you know?"

"He told me. That day he came here looking for you. He told me he wanted to kill you."

"Why? He never met me before. Why?"

"I don't know," she said. "He didn't tell me that."

Brody slowly pulled with his right hand, sliding the belt through the palm of his left.

"You're a lying goddamned slut," he said. "If he came to kill me, he wouldn't stop here and tell you. He works for me, him and his friend the half-breed. And they've had their chances to kill me if that's what they wanted. I'll teach you to lie to me."

He raised the belt over his head and swung it down

with all his force, again and again and again. Finally, his arm grew tired from the beating. He stopped and turned to look at the clock on the wall.

"I have to go clean up," he said. "I give a speech in an hour."

Brody had washed, shaved, and put on clean trousers and boots. He was about to select a clean shirt when he heard a knocking at his front door. General, still locked in a back room, set up another howl. He opened his mouth to yell at Susan to go see who was there, but before he did, he remembered the state he had left her in. It wouldn't do for anyone to see her like that. Not just now. It could be anyone out there. Maybe even someone from the capitol. He shouted at her anyway, but the order was changed.

"Shut that dog up," he said. He pulled on a fresh shirt and went to the door. When he opened it, there stood Edgar Wilhelm McDowell, his face bruised and caked with blood, his clothes torn and rumpled.

"Get out," said Brody and he started to shut the door. McDowell put a palm against the door to stop him.

"You'd better listen to me," he said, holding the folder up in front of Brody's face. "You'll be very interested in what I found in here."

Brody saw the name on the folder: Bobby Madison. He let go of the door and stepped back to allow McDowell to enter.

"What is it?" he asked. "I'm in a hurry. My speech is in fifteen minutes."

"You'll be lucky if you live through your speech," said McDowell. "I know who's trying to kill you. The same ones who killed Sneed and Bass and Olson."

"All right," said Brody. "Tell me. Who are they?"

"The same ones who got your four recruits."

"Who?" said Brody.

"The same ones who killed Potter and Cole."

"You fool," said Brody. "Potter and Cole were killed

by O'Rourke and that little gal, Wade's niece, Trish. You wrote it up yourself. Remember? It was all a mistake. O'Rourke and Trish."

"Trish who, Brody?" said the battered journalist. "Trish who? You're so almighty, so smart. What's her name?"

"I don't know her name," said Brody. "Nobody ever said her name. How would I know her name? Maybe it's Wade like her uncle. I don't know, and I don't give a damn. Now get out of here before I decide to finish what my boys started with you."

Brody turned his back on McDowell and headed back toward his room to finish dressing. McDowell took a menacing step toward the sheriff's back.

"It's Madison," he shouted. Brody stopped.

McDowell took another step toward Brody.

"Trish Madison," he said. "Madison. Madison. Madison."

Brody suddenly turned and ran for another door. He jerked it open with a shouted command.

"Get him, General."

The giant dog came out of the room with one great leap, snarling ferociously, his mouth gaping, fangs trailing saliva. He landed on McDowell's chest, his great weight and force carrying the horrified man back against the wall and on down to the floor. His fangs went for McDowell's throat, and the newspaperman screamed. It would be his last scream. Someone else would have to write the obituary.

Chapter 13

Robert D. and Pawnee were inside the Tanglefoot. At least they were only drinking coffee, Trish thought. She had seen enough of the Tanglefoot, so she left them there and went outside for some fresh air. But it didn't seem all that fresh outside, either. The street was crowded. Guns were being fired, and fireworks were being set off. Men on horseback ran up and down the street. Some celebration, she thought. It's more like a madhouse. Trish thought about walking over to Maude's Fine Food, but she didn't really know Maude and Claude well enough to just drop in on them for casual conversation. Besides, the place was probably full of customers anyway. Everyplace else in town was. Then she thought about going back to her room, but she rejected that idea, too. She would just wind up sitting there bored for a while, and then she would be back out on the street again. Besides, Robert D. might have something up his sleeve that he hadn't told her about yet. She had a feeling that something was going to happen that day. She couldn't give it a name, couldn't pin it down or provide a reason, but she had a feeling. Maybe it was just the atmosphere, the celebration, the madness in the air.

Trish walked aimlessly down the sidewalk, no particular destination in mind, and then she happened upon a small group of men gathered there in the street. The group seemed to be huddled around one man who was telling a story. She slowed down, then she stopped to listen.

"Hell, yes," said the man. "I was right there. I seen it all. I tell you, I seen a few gunfights in my time, but I never seen one to match that one."

"Was it just like it says in the book?" asked a man in the crowd.

"Well, sir," said the tale-teller, "the book told it pretty good, but it did make some mistakes. You see, that newspaper fella, he wasn't even there. He heard the story from someone who was, and he did a pretty good job of reporting it, but he did make some mistakes. If he'd a talked to me before he wrote that book, his story would a been even better than it is. But he never asked me."

"What time of day did it happen?"

"It was high noon. Exactly. It just happens that I had looked in the window of the barber shop over there and seen the clock. That's how I happen to know that for sure. I recollect that I had just told myself, so that's why I'm so damn hungry. You see, I hadn't realized that it was that late in the day already. So that's why I remember. It was high noon."

"And it happened right here?"

"Just about. Madison had just stepped out of Maude's over there. You see where Maude's is? Right over there. He had just come out of Maude's. I guess he'd et his lunch a mite early. He stepped out on the sidewalk there, and he just stood there kind of looking around, kind of like looking things over, you know?"

"Where was Brody?"

Trish stepped in closer. Her eyes were opened wide and her mouth was gaping. She wore a look at once fascinated and stunned.

"Brody just then came walking out of his office," continued the speaker. "He didn't even see Madison. At least if he did, he didn't give no indication. He was walking off in that direction there, like maybe he was going over

112

to the Tanglefoot. Then Madison called out to him. 'Brody,' he yells. 'Hey, Brody.' Brody stops in the street just over there. He turns and he looks. Then, 'Bobby Madison,' he says. Just like that. Real low and calm. 'Bobby Madison.' Like that.

"He walks toward Madison real slow, and he stops again just over there. Right about in the middle of the street. And, 'What do you want?' he says. 'I come for you,' says Madison. 'I aim to kill you.' Brody stays real calm. 'What for?' he says. Madison looks at him, real squinty-eyed, and he says, 'Because you wiped out my boys.' Brody looks him straight in the eyes, and, 'Madison,' he says, 'I don't want to have to kill you. Why don't you just climb on your horse,' he says, 'and ride out of town.'

"Then he turns to walk away. He actually turns his back on Bobby Madison, and that right after Madison has said, 'I aim to kill you.' He turns his back and starts to walk away, and Bobby Madison is snarling. I never seen a meaner face on a man. He's snarling, and he goes for his guns. He pulls them out, one in each hand, and he starts blasting away. He must have shot four or five shots, and one of them tore Brody's shirtsleeve. His left sleeve it was. Brody turns and draws at the same time. Oh, it was smooth, and he raises his big Colt and he fires one time. One shot. And it's dead center, and Bobby Madison drops dead right there in front of Maude's."

The man kept talking, but Trish didn't hear any more of what he said. She turned and walked back toward the Tanglefoot, and she walked as if in a daze. She was stunned by what she had heard. She remembered that she had had that fear once before, the fear that maybe Bobby had gone bad. She had known that he had killed, but she had always made excuses for him. He must have been forced into it. It must have been self-defense. But there had been the doubt. She hadn't seen Bobby for years, and he had been through the war. He could have gone bad. Then they had come to Drago, and they had not been able to find anyone who had seen the gunfight between Bobby and Brody. They had assumed, therefore, that there had been no gunfight. Now she had heard this man describe it. This man had witnessed it. Bobby had gone bad.

She walked into the Tanglefoot and found Robert D. and Pawnee sitting at a table with coffee cups in front of them. She stepped up to the table, but she did not sit down.

"Let's go," she said.

"Where?" asked Robert D.

"Let's get out of this town. Now."

"Now?" said Pawnee. "We ain't done."

"Trish," said Robert D, "what's the matter?"

"I want to get out of here," said Trish. "That's all."

She turned and ran out of the Tanglefoot, and Robert D. and Pawnee got up and went after her. She was almost back to the hotel before they caught her. Robert D. grabbed her by an arm and spun her around. He slammed her against the wall.

"What the hell's the matter with you?" he asked.

"We were wrong," said Trish. "Bobby asked for it. Bobby went bad. He started the fight, and he shot first, and he shot at Brody's back."

"Where did you get that?" asked Robert D.

"There was a man talking," she said. "He saw it all. I heard him."

"Where?"

"Right back there on the street."

"Let's go see him," said Pawnee.

"Come on," said Robert D. He took Trish by the arm and turned her back. "Is he still there?"

"I don't see him," she said. "Let's just leave."

"No," said Robert D. "We're going to have a talk with this man. Where is he?"

"I don't know," said Trish. "They were right there. They're gone now."

"They?"

"The man who saw it and the ones who were listening to him. They're gone.

"Well, he can't have gone far," said Pawnee. "It ain't a very big town. Let's find him."

They walked to the far end of the street and did not find the man there. They started back and looked in the Tanglefoot. It was crowded and it took them a while to search the faces, but he was not in there, either. They went back out.

"Where else could he have gone?" asked Robert D.

"Let's check Maude's," said Pawnee.

They crossed the street and looked through the window into Maude's Fine Food.

"There he is," said Trish.

"Which one?" said Robert D.

"Right over there against the wall with the red shirt on."

"Pawnee," said Robert D., "do you think that fellow might be willing to step out here for some conversation?"

"I'll ask him," said Pawnee.

"Real polite," said Robert D.

Pawnee walked into Maude's and went straight to the table of the red-shirted man.

"Partner," he said, "my name's O'Rourke. Me and two friends of mine would like to talk to you outside."

"I'm waiting for a meal, friend," said the man.

"Pawnee O'Rourke," said Pawnee with a slight edge to his voice.

"Oh, yeah," said the other. "I'm Sark. Olen Sark. I'll be glad to talk to you and your friends after I've et."

"Claude," said Pawnee.

Claude was bustling about, acting as waiter and cashier. He slowed down to respond to Pawnee.

"Is this man's meal about ready?"

"It'll be a few more minutes," said Claude. "We're awful busy."

"If he just steps outside for a couple of minutes with

115

me, you won't let anybody get his spot here, will you?"

"Well, I guess I can save it for him," said Claude.

Pawnee looked down at Sark and crossed his arms over his chest.

"You see?" he said. "You've got time and your dinner ain't ready yet."

Sark looked up. He saw Pawnee's reversed Remingtons and the big knife in the scout's belt. He also saw something fearsome in the man's eyes.

"Well," he said, "I guess just for a minute or two."

Pawnee followed Sark out the door and guided him over to where Robert D. and Trish waited on the sidewalk.

"This here is Mr. Olen Sark," he said. "Mr. Sark, these are my friends. Robert D. Wade and Trish."

Sark was nervous, but he tried to maintain his composure.

"Howdy, folks," he said. "What can I do for you?"

"I heard you telling the story of the gunfight between Bobby Madison and Sheriff Brody," said Trish.

"Oh," said Sark, beaming with pride. "That. Yeah, I seen it all right. Right here is where it happened. Madison was standing right over there just outside the door. Right where I just come out."

"At high noon," said Robert D.

"That's right," said Sark. "It was high noon."

"I wonder why Claude didn't see anything," said Robert D. "You said Bobby had just finished eating in there, right? That means the place was open. Claude was in there. How could he have missed a gunfight right at his front door?"

"Well," said Sark, "I don't know anything about that. I know what I seen, that's all. I can't answer for no one else. I was right over there. I—"

"Who else was on the street?" asked Robert D.

"Huh?"

"Who else was out here? Who else saw what you claim you saw?"

116

"Why, there was lots of folks out here. They all seen it."

"Who?"

"I don't know them. I didn't take no names. Hell, there was bullets a-flying."

"What did Bobby Madison look like?" Robert D asked.

"Uh . . . mean. Real mean. About the meanest-looking man I ever seen. He had two guns on, strapped down to his legs. Wore them real low."

"Was he a tall man," asked Robert D., "or short? Did he wear a beard or not? Heavy? Skinny? How old was he?"

"I don't know. Hell, man, when bullets is flying, you don't notice them kind of things. What's this all about? Leave me alone. I got to go back inside. My dinner's about ready by now."

Sark tried to leave, but Pawnee took hold of his arm and gripped it tight.

"Mister," said Robert D., "this is real important to us, especially to this young girl here. I can't tell you why, so you just take my word that it's real important. Now, I want the truth."

"I seen what I seen," said Sark.

"I think you're a big bag of wind," said Robert D. "And that's all right. You like to tell tales, don't you? You like to have a crowd around you listening to what you've got to say. I think that you read that book that's for sale all over town, and when all these strangers started coming in, you decided that you could tell a big lie to entertain folks. No harm in it. Am I right?"

"Now, see here, mister, you got no call to pick on me."

"Just tell me the truth, and that'll be the end of it," said Robert D. "I ain't going to kill you for telling tall tales, and I ain't even going to hurt you. I won't even spread the word that you're a windbag. I just want you to tell me the truth right now. Just between us right here. It won't go no further."

"I think your dinner's ready," said Pawnee.

"Please," said Trish.

"There's no harm in it," said Sark. "No harm. Just telling tales. That's all."

"Is that the truth?" asked Robert D.

"You ain't going to tell?"

"I promise."

Sark looked at Trish and at Pawnee.

"I won't tell anyone," said Trish.

"Me neither," said Pawnee. "I ain't going to say anything."

"Is that the truth?" asked Robert D. "Is it the truth that you was just telling tales? You never saw the gunfight?"

Sark sighed, a sigh of defeat, and his shoulders sagged. He looked down at the sidewalk as he spoke.

"I never seen it," he said. "I was just telling tales. Can I go back inside now?"

"I'll walk you back," said Pawnee.

As Pawnee walked back inside with Sark, Trish turned away from Robert D. She paced a few steps, then turned and paced back.

"I should have known," she said. "I feel like a damn fool."

Robert D. pulled her to him and hugged her close for a minute.

"Don't worry about it, honey," he said. "Forget it."

Inside Maude's, Sark sat down at his place. The meal was waiting for him. Pawnee pulled out a chair and sat down close beside him.

"One more thing, Mr. Sark," he said. "If you tell that tale again, anywhere, anytime, I'll cut your belly open."

Chapter 14

Brody pulled on his jacket and checked his appearance in the long mirror in the hallway. General was once again secured in the back room. It was time for his speech but Brody's mind was no longer on it, nor on the twenty-fifth birthday of Drago. Susan had not lied to him after all. It was Robert D. Wade and his companions who were after him. Wade and O'Rourke were professional killers, good at their trade, and the girl was, from what Brody had heard, pretty deadly herself. The situation called for immediate attention. On his way out the front door, Brody paused only briefly for a glance at what was left of Edgar Wilhelm McDowell. He stepped out on the porch, then paused. He had thought he was going to town, but Wade and his killers were in there somewhere. He would be safer at home. There was General to protect him, and if he could get his entire force of deputies around the house, not even Robert D. Wade and his partners could get to him. He walked around the house and fought his way through the crowd of curious tourists until he had gotten to Sand.

"Hiram," he said, "get rid of all these people."

"Get rid of them?" said Sand.

"Now."

There were a few protests but soon the crowd was gone, and Brody called Sand and Hogan over to him.

They stood by the fence near where the two deputies had tied their horses. Brody had walked to the house, so those two were the only horses around.

"Hiram," said Brody, "I want you to mount up and get into town and get everybody out here. Not Wade and O'Rourke, but everybody else. I want them mounted and well armed. Tell them to bring everything they got."

"Mr. Brody," said Sand, "Harper and Jones is on duty at the Tanglefoot, and—"

"I don't give a damn if they're guarding the virgin Mary's tomb," said Brody. "Get them all out here like I said, and hurry."

"Yes, sir," said Sand. He jumped the fence and mounted up, racing toward town. Brody turned to Hogan.

"After a while," he said, "when I tell you to, I want you to do something for me. It's a special job. I don't want nobody else to even know about it. There'll be a bonus in it for you, you understand?"

"Sure, Mr. Brody. What is it?"

"Mr. McDowell wandered into my house a little while ago without waiting to be invited. You know how my dog is. Ed never had a chance. I got the dog locked up now, and I want you to get poor old Ed out of the house. Take him out somewhere way off. I don't want to have to explain what happened to him in there."

"You just say when, Mr. Brody," said Hogan. "I'll take care of it for you."

Susan was watching through a window in back of the house when Brody had the yard cleared of all the tourists. She knew then that he was up to something. Then she saw him send Sand away. He never left the house with only one guard. Of course, he was out there in back himself with Hogan. Still, she thought, he's up to something. She knew, too, that it was time for his big speech, and all of a sudden he was seemingly unconcerned about

120

that. Susan wondered if it was because of McDowell. She had heard the commotion and had looked out long enough to see what was happening. Then she had turned away from the sight in horror. But she couldn't imagine that Brody would let anything like that interfere with his big moment. He had been planning this speech for weeks. She had been forced any number of times to sit and listen to him practice it. It was a dreadful, pompous speech, but she had dutifully told him that it was marvelous and would undoubtedly make him the next governor. And now he was ignoring it. The crowd was gathering at the stand, waiting for his appearance, and he was standing in the backyard with Hogan. Something was up. While she watched, Sand came riding back. Behind him were Jones and Harper. Soon the last three of the uniformed deputies, Earl Collins, Chub Collins, and Pete Watts, rode up to the yard. All seven deputies tied their horses to the picket fence and gathered around Brody in the backyard. Susan made a quick decision. She had to get out.

She didn't want to look at McDowell's remains, but as she moved toward the front door, she couldn't control her gaze. In spite of her desire, her eyes moved in that direction. As she cringed at the sight Susan noticed a folder there on the floor beside the body, its contents scattered. She wondered what it might be, if it might be important. Could it be what had gotten McDowell killed? If so, could it be used against her husband? She gathered up the papers as quickly as she could and rushed out the door. Moving around the house, she stayed close to the south wall. The seven horses were tied along the fence on that side, and the nearest had worked his way around until he was standing almost beside the house, partially hidden from view to those out back. Brody had gathered his men on the other side of the yard. Her heart pounding in desperation, she reached for the reins. What if someone saw her? Brody would surely kill her for this. She undid the reins from the picket

121

fence and pulled on them, bringing the horse to her, completely out of view of Brody and the deputies. But they were out of her view, too, and she imagined one of them running across the lawn to suddenly jump out at her. Susan mounted the horse clumsily. She was not much of a rider to begin with, and she was clutching the folder in her right hand. In addition, her whole body ached from the savage beating she had received at her husband's hands. But she mounted the horse and got him turned toward town, then she kicked him viciously in the sides and raced him toward the main street.

Maximillian Sweet was Drago's only undertaker. He was also the official master of ceremonies for the formalities of the opening day there at the newly constructed platform. The crowd that had gathered was huge and it was beginning to grow restless. Sheriff Brody was to be the first speaker. The smell of barbecue floated through the air, but no one would eat until after the speechmaking. People were starting to yell and taunt. It seemed to Sweet as if they were becoming a threat to his very safety. He didn't know what to do. He had nothing to say without a speaker to introduce. He was afraid to tell them to go ahead and eat. He felt that he lacked the authority to make such a decision. Finally, he set out for the blue house at a run. He noticed a rather disheveled-looking woman riding a horse toward town, but he was too worried about his own problem to pay her much attention. The whole town was packed with crazy people, anyway. Sweet reached the picket fence out of breath, but somehow he managed a shout.

"Sheriff Brody," he called. "Sheriff."

"Go on back, Max," said Brody. "We got an emergency here."

"We've got one down there, too," said Sweet. "That crowd's getting unruly. They want your speech."

Sweet thought that would sound better than telling

Brody the crowd wanted to eat. Brody stalked over to the fence.

"You make the speech, Max," he said. "Take care of it for me."

"Sheriff," said Sweet, "they won't let me. They hooted me off the platform. You've got to come. The governor's down there, too."

Suddenly Brody's political ambitions struggled back to the forefront of his conscious mind.

"All right, Max," he said. "You go on back down there and introduce me. I'll be coming right behind you. Go on."

As Sweet headed reluctantly back toward the stand, Brody waved his men to him.

"I got to go down there and make that damn speech," he said. "It would be a perfect time for those killers to try for me. You're all coming with me. You know who to watch for. Let's go."

A couple of deputies headed for the horses, but Brody stopped them.

"We'll walk down," he said. It was a long walk, but the view from where the crowd waited was unobstructed. Brody's approach, with the deputies behind him, would be dramatic. He turned to Hogan. "You go take care of that other little job," he said, then began the march toward the platform. Hogan watched them until they were a ways off from the house, then he walked around to the front and went inside. He stopped and stared at the mangled corpse there on the floor.

"My God," he said. General began snarling and barking from behind the door to the back room, and Hogan jumped in fright. A chill ran through his entire body. He reminded himself that Brody had assured him the dog was securely locked away. He looked around and figured out which door the beast was behind, then he walked hurriedly to another door. It was closed, and he was afraid to try it even though he had already located the dog. He looked at another door. It was not quite shut.

123

That one should be safe. He tried it and found that it led to the bedroom. He needed something in which to wrap the body, so he entered the room and jerked the huge quilt off the bed. He would wrap the body in that, load it onto one of the horses, and take it out of town somewhere, probably across the river to the east and into the mesquite thicket that began there, maybe even beyond to the foothills. He wondered how big a bonus Brody would give him for this special job.

While Hogan was thus engaged in his grisly task, Sweet was just finishing his introduction of Brody, who was approaching from behind the crowd. The people, seeing the armed guard that accompanied the sheriff, had become very decorous.

"And now, my friends," squeaked Sweet at the top of his voice, "I give you the man who has brought our town to its present state of peace and tranquility, its present level of civilization; the man who killed Bobby Madison, Sheriff Phil Brody."

Sweet made a wild gesture in Brody's direction, and there was thunderous applause from the crowd. The sheriff took off his hat and waved it over his head as he mounted the platform. The deputies stayed behind the crowd and fanned out. Brody, from his vantage point on the platform, scanned the faces out in front of him for any sign of Robert D., Pawnee, or Trish. Seeing none, he relaxed a little, and his mind went back to fame and fortune.

"My friends," he roared "welcome to Drago's twenty-fifth birthday party."

"Anyone want to go listen to Brody's speech?" asked Pawnee. The street had gone from wild and dangerous to almost deserted.

"It'd make me puke," said Trish.

"Let's go back inside and get a drink," said Robert D. Just then he saw Susan. He blinked his eyes in disbelief. At first he thought it must be someone who looked mightily like Susan, for he had never seen her look quite like that before. She was riding a horse, and her clothes were ripped and wrinkled. In fact, they barely performed their basic function of covering her body. Her hair was wildly unkempt, and she had a general frantic manner about her. She was looking up and down the street when she spotted Robert D. and came riding toward him. As she got closer, Robert D. could see the blood and the bruises. He ran to meet her.

"Susan," he said, "what's that son of a bitch done to you?"

He helped her down out of the saddle. Pawnee had come running right behind him, and he took hold of the horse's reins.

"There's no time," said Susan. "I had to tell him."

"Had to tell him what?" asked Trish, who had arrived on the scene only slightly behind Pawnee.

"I told him that it was you who wanted to kill him. I'm sorry. I didn't think he believed me, but then Mr. McDowell showed up and Phil set General on him. It was awful. McDowell dropped this."

Robert D. was holding Susan up, so Trish took the folder from her hand.

"This is a file on Bobby," she said.

"He's got all the deputies with him," said Susan. "All of them together. He's never done that before."

Robert D. shot a quick glance toward Pawnee.

"Go get the horses ready," he said. "Take her with you. Susan, you'll have to ride some more. Can you do it?"

"Yes," she said.

He helped her back into the saddle.

"Go with Pawnee," he said. "We'll be with you in a minute."

As Pawnee led the horse that was carrying Susan toward the stable, Robert D. and Trish hurried to their rooms in the Grand Hotel. They put their saddle rolls back together and left again. Pawnee met them in the street. They strapped on the rolls, mounted up, and rode out of town toward the south.

Chapter 15

"My friends, the days of the wild West are numbered. Here in Drago, they have ended. Civilization is here, and civilization will spread over the entire West. And paving the way for civilization has not been an easy task. Some of us have risked our lives on a daily basis, so that the West might be made a safe place for the rest of you to raise your children and live quiet, peaceful, and productive lives."

Brody droned on. He had been talking for twenty minutes, and some in the audience were beginning to wonder if there would ever be an end to it. The aroma of barbecued beef in the air was beginning to be torture for the hungriest in the crowd, and even the few who were staunch supporters of Brody were worried that the sheriff might at last be losing it. The man's pomposity and arrogance were showing through too clearly. A show, at least, of humility on a public occasion, they thought, would be tasteful and appropriate. Some firecrackers went off somewhere in the background. A few of the younger children had stood it as long as they could and had returned to their own kind of celebration.

"When I killed Bobby Madison," Brody continued, "I did not do so for the glory that would come my way. Bobby Madison was a notorious outlaw and killer. He was a menace to this community or any other community he might have ventured into at some later date. He was a threat to our lives and property, to the honor of our women, and to the safety and well-being of our children."

More firecrackers popped somewhere behind Brody.

"And what's more, ladies and gentlemen, my good friends, what's more, he was an immediate and dire threat to my own life. Bobby Madison knew, in spite of his own demented brain, he knew that in Drago, in our town, I represented law and order. Therefore he knew that as long as I was alive, I stood in his way and he would not be allowed to ply his evil trade. He came for me with intent to kill or to cower me into complacency or to run me out of town. It didn't matter to him one way or the other, so long as I was out of his way and he was left free to follow his nefarious ways."

A bottle rocket sailed high into the air and exploded, it appeared to the crowd, directly above Brody's head.

"I could have thought first of my own safety. I could have fled. I could have comfortably avoided my duty to my community and ultimately to the entire West and the future of this fine country of ours, but I did not do that. I could not turn my back on you, my friends, the fine people of Drago. I faced Bobby Madison, right out here on this street at high noon, and when he snarled at me and slapped leather, I calmly drew my revolver, and with bullets whistling past my head, I shot him dead."

Pawnee reined in his paint pony only about halfway out the road toward the Van Tuyl store. Robert D. and the others stopped to see what Pawnee was up to.

"You all go on," said Pawnee. "I'm going to double back a ways and cover our tracks. We don't want to get them Dutchmen in any kind of trouble. I'll catch up to you later."

Robert D., Trish, and Susan rode on toward the Van Tuyls' placed, while Pawnee headed back toward Drago.

"Hang on, Susan," said Robert D. "We're about halfway there."

"I'm all right," said Susan, but both Robert D. and Trish could see that she was lying. They rode one on either side of the battered woman in case she should need some help. Somehow Susan managed to stay in the saddle, but when they arrived at the Van Tuyls' place, she almost fell. Robert D. grabbed her and helped her down. Trish eyed Susan with mixed feelings. She still did not like this woman, perhaps only because she was the wife of Phil Brody. Yet she could not help but feel pity for her in her present condition. And they did have a common enemy. Susan was Brody's wife, yes, but it was now apparent that all that meant was that she was desperate to escape. They helped her inside and found her a comfortable chair back in the living quarters. Lisa ran the men out so that she and Trish could bathe Susan's body and dress her wounds. Robert D. and Dutch walked outside.

"A man that would do that to his own wife," said Dutch, "he's an animal."

"I don't know of any animal that acts like that," said Robert D. "Dutch, we been found out by Brody."

"How?"

"That ain't important. What's important is that we need to hide out somewhere."

"You're welcome—" Dutch began, but Robert D. cut him off.

"It can't be here, Dutch. We don't want to put you and your missus in any danger. I said we been found out, but that don't include you. Brody don't know nothing about you even being acquainted with us."

"I want to help," said Dutch, "and so does Lisa. We're not afraid."

"I know that, and you've already helped. You're helping now, and you can be even more help, especially if Brody don't know that you're helping. Pawnee dropped back a while ago to cover our tracks so we won't be followed out here to your place. I only stopped by here mainly because of Susan."

"All right," said Dutch. "We'll get you some food together, some supplies. I do know a place. The old goatman's place. That's what everybody called him. He died a few months back, and the goats have mostly been picked

129

up by folks or killed. There's a few of them still running wild and hanging out around the old place. It's almost due east of here. You ride straight east from the house. You'll come to the river. It's an easy crossing. It ain't much of a river. Just on the other side the mesquite thicket starts. If you can find your way through that, you'll be in the foothills. There's a trail that leads on up in there. Probably pretty well grown up by now. There's no one out there since the goatman died. Follow the trail, and you'll find his house. It's only a couple hours ride from here. I'll check on you every now and then."

"No," said Robert D. "Let us do the checking. You stay right here."

Dutch sighed and looked back toward the building that was both house and store. The women had not yet made an appearance nor called out to the men. He turned back toward Robert D.

"Smoke?" he asked.

"Sure."

Dutch pulled the makings out of his pocket and handed them to Robert D., who soon had a cigarette rolled. He gave them back to Van Tuyl, who rolled himself one, then reached into his pocket for matches. As they lit their smokes, Dutch looked back toward Drago.

"Here comes Pawnee," he said.

To the great relief of all his nearly captive audience, Brody finally finished his speech, and the crowd was unleashed on the free food. The noise level in Drago increased immediately and dramatically. Brody gathered his deputies around him once more.

"I want you two to stay with me," he said, indicating Jones and Harper. "The rest of you fan out and search this whole damn town. I want Robert D. Wade, Trish Madison, and Pawnee O'Rourke either dead or locked up in my jail. You got that? I want it done before dark tonight."

The deputies looked back longingly at the free food line and went reluctantly on their way. They divided into two groups, each taking one side of Drago's main street, and began methodically checking each building along the way.

"Come on," said Brody, waving at his two bodyguards to follow. He led them directly to the Grand Hotel. Purlie almost came to attention behind the counter when he saw the three lawmen enter the lobby.

"Sheriff Brody," he said. "What can I do for you?"

"Has Robert D. Wade and his two outlaw companions got rooms here?" asked Brody.

"Yes, sir," said Purlie, "they have. Uh . . . outlaws?"

"Which rooms?" demanded Brody.

"First two on the right at the top of the stairs," said Purlie.

Brody stomped his way up the stairs, followed closely by Jones and Harper. Once in the hallway upstairs, however, he stood back.

"Check them out," he ordered.

Jones and Harper drew their revolvers and looked at each other. Jones stepped forward and tested the first door. He was surprised to find it unlocked. He pushed the door open and waited. Then he rushed into the room with Harper just behind. No one was there. They repeated the procedure in the next room, with the same results. When Brody was sure that the rooms were unoccupied, he went in to look them over. There were no clothes, no personal belongings.

"Damn," he said, and he stomped back down the stairs. Jones and Harper were again right behind him.

"They're gone," Brody shouted at Purlie.

"But they didn't check out," said Purlie. "They haven't paid their bill."

"Add that to their list of crimes," said the sheriff, heading for the door. Once outside, he kept walking. The deputies followed, not knowing where they were going. Eventually, they wound up at the livery stable. There they found that the trio's horses were gone. Pawnee O'Rourke had come for them that very morning. He had paid the bill.

"Looks like they've left town, boss," said Jones.

131

Brody leaned back against the wall and pulled out a cigar from his pocket. Jones quickly found a match, struck it against the wall, and held it up for Brody. Brody puffed until the match flame was about to burn Jones's fingers. He leaned back again, and Jones shook the match out and threw it down.

"Yeah," said Brody, "it looks that way. We'll let the search continue just to make sure. If they have gotten out of town, we're going after them. I want those three."

Trish came running out of the Van Tuyl house to join Robert D. and Dutch. Pawnee had arrived by then and was standing with the other two men.

"How is she?" asked Robert D.

"Oh, she'll be all right," said Trish. "He beat her up pretty bad, but it seems to be mostly cuts and bruises. No serious damage, I think. Look."

She held out the folder that Susan had been carrying.

"It's a file on Bobby from the newspaper office," she added.

Robert D. took the file and opened it up.

"Why did she bring this along, I wonder," said Robert D.

"You can read through it if you want," said Trish, "but I already read it, and I'll tell you why. We're identified in there. You and me and Pawnee. That's why she brought it. To show us. That newspaperman must have taken it to Brody's house."

"Well," said Robert D. "that doesn't change anything for us. It does mean that Susan won't have to feel so bad about giving us away. Brody had this information here just a little while after she broke down and told him about me, so what she said didn't matter in the long run."

He handed the folder back to Trish.

"I don't know what all's in there," he said, "but you might want to keep some of it, or you might want to make sure it's all burned. It's up to you."

Trish took the folder and nodded.

"I'll go and see if she's ready to travel," she said.

Some miles south of Drago, Hogan rode up out of the river. He was leading a horse with an empty saddle. He had crossed the river to dispose of the remains of McDowell somewhere in the vast mesquite thicket. No one will ever find him there, he thought, or even if they do, there won't be nothing left but bones by then. He rode on toward the road that would take him back into Drago, but by the time he reached it, he wanted a drink. He had ridden so far out of town that he was closer to Van Tuyl's store than to Drago. He decided that he would go on out there before returning to town. What Brody didn't know wouldn't hurt him. He turned his horse south.

Up ahead at the store, Pawnee had lagged behind once again to cover the tracks of his companions. He had let them get a good start on him because he had wanted a cup of Lisa Van Tuyl's coffee. He had just climbed into the saddle on his paint pony when he saw the rider, who was leading a second horse, coming along the road toward the store. He backed the paint slowly around the far edge of the building and, leaning forward in the saddle, peered around the corner. The rider came closer, and Pawnee recognized the uniform of one of Brody's deputies. Real handy of him to dress them up like that, he said to himself. He reached down and eased the Winchester repeating rifle out of its scabbard, and he worked the lever to load a bullet into the chamber. Hogan was almost in front of the building when Pawnee nudged the paint pony and rode out to confront him, rifle in hand.

"Hold it right there," said Pawnee.

Hogan stopped his horse and raised his hands a little. The Winchester was aimed at his chest. It would be foolish to try to draw.

"I just stopped by for a drink," he said. "What's the problem?"

"Get on down then," said Pawnee. "I'll buy your drink."

Hogan's horse was stamping and fidgeting a bit, and the deputy allowed him to move around seemingly without purpose until the animal's right side was toward Pawnee.

"All right," he said, and swung his right leg over to drop to the ground with the horse between him and Pawnee. He had allowed the riderless horse to roam free. His shotgun hung from a strap on the left side of the saddle. He slipped it loose, dropped to one knee, and swung the barrel up under the horse's neck. Pawnee fired and his shot smashed Hogan's left clavicle, but the deputy's finger had already been tightening on the trigger of his gun. The blast went off, but the aim was spoiled. The shot went high and wide, but several scattered pellets tore into Pawnee's left arm and shoulder. He shouted in pain and anger, chambered another shell, and fired again. His second shot tore through Hogan's chest, and the man crumpled into a ball. Dutch Van Tuyl came running out of the store. He looked around and quickly took in the scene.

"Pawnee," he said, "you all right?"

"Ah," said Pawnee, "took some shot in the arm. He ain't doing so good, though."

"I can see that," said Dutch. "Come on back in and let Lisa see what she can do about that arm."

"It'll be all right," said Pawnee. "I've got to get this son of a bitch out of your yard."

Lisa had appeared in the doorway by that time.

"You get in here," she said.

"Go on," said Dutch. "I'll load him on his horse for you while Lisa's taking care of that. Then you can take him off with you."

Pawnee stretched his neck to look down the road toward Drago. There was no sign of any other riders. With a loud sigh of resignation, he climbed down off his pony.

Chapter 16

Robert D. found the trail that Dutch had told them about, but in the days since the death of the goatman, it had become little more than a goat path down through the hills and the thicket to the river. The river crossing had been no problem, the water at its deepest barely reaching the riders' boots. Susan rode uncomfortably because of her cuts and bruises. She was dressed in some men's clothing that Trish had given her. As the goat path wound its way on up into the hills, it became walled by large boulders. Robert D. took particular note of one high boulder with a flat top, which towered above them as they crested a hill. A billy goat stood watch on it. On the other side of the path were other similar rocks, though not as high as that one. They rode on to the top of the hill, and for a short distance the ground leveled off. Then the path snaked on up another steep hill. At the top of that one they found the old goatherd's house.

"This must be the place," said Robert D.

He stayed in the saddle for a moment, looking around and listening. At first the silence seemed overwhelming. A slight breeze stirred the vegetation on the hillsides. Then in the distance a goat bleated. Robert D. swung down out of the saddle, and the noise of the creaking leather seemed louder than normal. He allowed the reins to trail on the ground while he walked up to the door, which was standing open, and stepped into the house. It was completely furnished, but it was still a shambles. Everything was covered with a thick layer of dust through which could be seen little trails of goat prints. He stepped back outside.

"It's okay," he said, and he walked over to help Susan down off her horse. "You two go on inside. I'll take care of the horses."

Trish and Susan went to the house, and Robert D. walked the horses around back. There he found the remains of a small corral. He unsaddled the horses and turned them into the corral. He then set about the task of repairing the fence. It was a simple rail fence, and the rails were all there. He only had to pick them up and put them back in place. With the horses more or less secured, he went back into the house. Trish and Susan were dusting off the furniture.

"Housecleaning?" he asked.

"We don't know how long we'll be here, do we?" said Susan.

"No," said Robert D. "I guess we don't."

Back in Drago, Brody's deputies had finished their search of the town. They had all gathered once again in the Tanglefoot, where Brody held court from his reserved table. His bottle of special brandy was in front of him, and he held a glass in his right hand. Six men in uniform stood before him, six of his original twelve. It was getting late, and Hogan had not returned. Brody had decided that he would not. Either things were getting too hot for him and he had hightailed it out for parts unknown, or Wade and those bastards had gotten him. The latter, he thought, was most likely, as Hogan had not yet collected his promised bonus. He tossed down his drink and refilled the glass.

"They've got away," he said, "and I want them brought back."

He paused, assessing his situation. Robert D. Wade was no dummy. What if Brody were to send all the deputies, the six remaining ones, out on the trail? He would be left alone in Drago to defend himself. Then Wade and his gang could slip back into town and kill him. Well, he wouldn't fall for that. He wouldn't send all six men out, only half of them. Yes. Three would be enough. He could take the other three and go back to his house. There was nothing around the house — no hills, no trees — just flat prairie. He could easily see anyone approaching from any direction. There Brody, the three deputies, and General would be able to fend off any attack by Wade, O'Rourke, and the girl. He took another sip of brandy and set down the glass.

"Collins, Watts, Moss," he said. "You three get mounted up. They rode out of town in some direction or other. They had to leave tracks. Go find them. Find out which way they went. When you've found out, come back and tell me. Once we got them located, we can all go out after them. I'll be at my house when you get back."

When Pawnee arrived at the goatherd's house, he found supper almost prepared from the supplies Dutch had provided them with. The coffee was made, and Trish poured him a cup.

"What happened?" asked Robert D. when he noticed the blood stains on Pawnee's shirt. The scout had ridden up to the house leading two extra horses.

"Aw, I run into one of them deputies from Drago," said Pawnee. "He got the worst of it."

"Where at?"

"Right there at Dutch's place. He come riding up just as I was fixing to leave. I offered to buy him a drink, but the son of a bitch sprayed me some. I left him down in them mesquites."

"How's your arm?" asked Trish.

"It's starting to get a little stiff," said Pawnee, "but it'll heal."

"This deputy," said Robert D, "he was alone?"

"Yeah. I covered up your tracks here, too. Nobody won't find us here."

Robert D. walked to the door and opened it. He stood there in the doorway, staring off down the path.

"You know," he said, "it might not be so bad if they did."

137

Pawnee leaned back in his chair and raised his eyebrows quizzically at Robert D.'s back. Trish and Susan stopped what they were doing to listen. Robert D. had stopped talking.

"Well?" said Pawnee.

"Well, what?"

"You just going to leave it at that?"

Robert D. turned around, closing the door behind him. He walked over to the table where Pawnee sat drinking his coffee, and he pulled out a chair and sat down.

"Riding up here on that little goat trail," he said, "did you notice that spot just at the top of a hill, big boulders on each side? On the left the tallest one was kind of flat-topped. A billy goat was up there kind of standing guard when we passed by."

"He was still there when I come up," said Pawnee.

"There don't seem to be any other way to get here."

"Nope."

"How many men does Brody have left?" asked Robert D.

"I count six," said Pawnee.

"Count Brody," said Robert D. "That makes seven. If they was to move against us up here and we waited for them where that billy goat was standing guard, we could take them . . . easy."

"Real easy," said Pawnee.

"Let's sleep on it," said Robert D. "In the morning, I'll ride back down to see Dutch again."

"Right now," said Susan, "supper's ready."

"And home cooked," said Pawnee. "Well, bring it on."

When Brody arrived at the blue house, he left Jones and Harper on the front porch. Sand was sent to the backyard, and the sheriff went on inside. General had set up a howl when he heard the footsteps on the porch. He was still locked up in the back room. Brody began shouting orders.

"Susan, shut that damn dog up."

Not receiving an immediate response, he went to the door behind which General lurked and banged on it with his fist.

"Shut up in there," he shouted. "General, shut up."

The dog obeyed, and Brody turned back into the living room.

"Susan," he called. "Susan. Get out here."

Still there was no response. He stalked to the bedroom and jerked open the door. He thrust his head into the room to look around. She was not there.

"Susan."

His voice grew louder as his anger increased and his patience diminished. He hurried through the house, checking each room. She was gone. He went to the front door and opened it.

"My wife is gone," he said.

"Mr. Brody," said Jones, "one of the horses we had tied out here a while ago is missing, too. I mean, besides the two that Hogan took when he went riding out."

"Why the hell didn't you tell me before?"

"I'm sorry, Mr. Brody," said Jones. "I guess there was just too many things happening."

Brody stepped out onto the porch and stood, his hands on his hips. He stared out into the dimming sky. It was getting quiet again, the celebrants having mostly worn themselves out. They had been going strong since early morning. Now and then the night stillness was broken by the sound of a string of firecrackers going off, and once a bottle rocket exploded in the sky back down over the Tanglefoot.

"She's with them," he said. His voice was low. Wade, he thought. Robert D. Wade. Susan has run off with Robert D. Wade. By God, when I get my hands on her again, she'll wish I'd killed her before I'm through.

"What was that, Mr. Brody?" asked Jones.

"Huh? Oh, I said Wade and them has kidnapped my wife. They stole that horse and kidnapped my wife. I hope we can get them alive, boys. I want to see them hang."

"Riders coming," said Harper. All three men walked to the south edge of the porch to see who was coming. Three riders approached from the direction of Drago. Brody jerked out his pistol, and Jones and Harper held their shotguns ready. The riders came closer.

"It's Collins and them," said Brody. He holstered his gun and waited until the three deputies had ridden up to the porch. "Well?" he asked.

"There ain't no tracks," said Collins. "It's kind of eerie. It's like ain't nobody rode out of Drago—ever. Not in any direction."

"Hogan rode out," said Brody, "leading an extra horse."

"He didn't leave no tracks," said Watts. "Nobody else did, either."

"Damn it," shouted Brody. He paced the length of his porch, paused, then paced back again. "All right," he said. "There's six of you. I want two men here on the porch, two in the backyard, and one on each side of the house. I want all directions watched at all times. You got that?"

"Yes, sir," said Collins.

"I'm going inside. Anybody comes toward this house from any direction, you let me know right away, you hear? Nobody comes close to this house. Nobody."

Brody went inside and slammed the door. General barked.

"Shut up," Brody shouted. He went to his liquor cabinet and poured himself a brandy. Then he sat down in his favorite chair. They're out there somewhere, he thought. I don't know where they are but they're out there, and they mean to come after me.

There was one old cot in the goatman's house, but it was serviceable. Because of her bruises, Susan was assigned the cot. Trish made herself a pallet on the floor just inside the door, and Robert D. and Pawnee took their bedrolls outside. Pawnee bedded down by the corral out back, and Robert D. found himself a spot near the trail in front of the house. It was a dark night and quiet, and everyone had been in bed for at least a half hour. They should have been asleep. But Trish heard the cot creak when Susan got up. She pretended to be asleep, but she heard the soft footsteps on the old floor as the other woman made her way to the front door. With slightly opened eyes, even in the darkness, she

140

watched as the shadowy figure moved through the doorway and vanished into the night outside. Trish knew what the bitch was up to, and she was both resentful and disgusted.

It took her a little while to locate him in the dark, but Susan found Robert D. She stood there in the dirt, her feet bare, a blanket wrapped tightly around her, looking down on him.

Robert D. was a light sleeper. He had both heard and seen her approach. He was lying on his back, looking at her, but Susan didn't know that. Her eyes were not as accustomed to the dark as were his, and all she could see down on the ground was his outline. Finally, she spoke, her voice soft and low, a harsh yet feminine whisper.

"Robert D.," Susan said, "are you awake?"

"I'm awake," he said.

She loosed her grip on the blanket and allowed it to drop to the ground around her feet and ankles, and she was there before him naked. It was too dark to see the cuts and bruises. He saw only the outline, the near perfect figure, the graceful body curves. He had felt them before, more than once, but those trysts had been marred by the fact that they had taken place in Brody's house. Out here in the clean night air in the hills, she didn't really seem to be Brody's wife. The man was a brute, and she had left him. As far as Robert D. was concerned, that constituted divorce. Here and now she was just Susan, and she was beautiful and desirable. He thought about the beating she had suffered and the long ride she had endured, the bruises and abrasions on her lovely body.

"Susan," he said, "do you think you should be doing this? After — ?"

"I'm not hurt so bad I can't make love to you," she said, and she stepped across his reclining body and stood for a moment, straddling him. Slowly, she lowered herself to her knees until he felt her weight press against his pelvis. He reached up with both his hands and touched her breasts, gently, tenderly, carefully.

"Don't be afraid of hurting me, Robert D.," Susan said, and she leaned forward to press her open lips against his.

141

Inside the house Trish sat up, leaning against the wall, her arms folded across her breasts, an angry scowl on her face. She could feel the agitation growing from the pit of her stomach, and the anger was causing her limbs to tremble ever so slightly there in the darkness of the goatman's cabin.

Chapter 17

Claude finally got a bit of relief. There were only two customers sitting at tables inside Maude's Fine Food. He sat down with a cup of coffee, and a minute later, Maude came out of the kitchen and joined him.

"I'm worn out," she said.

"It's been a long day," said Claude. "Busy day."

"If we had one day a week like this, we could retire in a couple of years."

"If we lived through it," said Claude.

One of the customers got up to leave, paying Claude on the way out. That left only Alfie Dolan, who had just eaten enough for four ordinary men. Alfie got up with his coffee cup and moved over to join Claude and his wife. Maude got the pot and refilled the cups.

"That was just fine, Maude," said Dolan. "Maude's Fine Food."

"Thank you, Alfie. I'm glad you like it. Did you get enough?"

"It'll last me a little while," said Dolan. "Sure a lot of folks in town."

"The big celebration has drawed them in like flies," said Claude.

"Yeah," said Dolan. He stared into his coffee cup, musing, as if he had something more serious on his mind. "There's some strange things going on in town," he said.

"You noticed?"

"This has always been a strange town," said Maude. "At least, ever since Brody showed up."

"Yeah," said Dolan. "But . . . well, you know that fellow that I had a fight with? The half-breed that whipped me?"

"O'Rourke," said Claude.

"Yeah. Him and his friends."

"Yeah," said Claude.

"What about them?" said Maude. "They seem like pretty nice folks to me. They've been eating in here ever since they hit town."

"There was talk around town that Brody hired them on as some kind of special deputies," said Dolan.

"They didn't seem to me like the type to work for Brody," said Claude. "I can't figure that."

"Other things have been happening," said Dolan. "Brody's men tore up the newspaper office and beat up McDowell. Beat him up pretty bad."

"I heard about that," said Claude.

"It's awful," said Maude. "Just awful."

"The same thing could happen to us if we crossed Brody," said Claude. "We all know that. We've known it all along."

"Yeah," said Dolan, "but it seems like it's getting worse all of a sudden. Nobody's seen McDowell since just a little while after he was beat up. He's just gone. And then some friends of mine said they seen Mrs. Brody ride out of town with O'Rourke and his friends. Brody's spread it around that they kidnapped her, but my friends said it sure didn't look like no kidnaping to them."

"That's when them damn deputies went tearing all over town, searching every building," said Claude.

"They came through here like a herd of wild horses," said Maude. "No-good, ornery bunch of coyotes."

She stood up, stalked over to the table where Dolan had eaten his meal, and began clearing away the dishes with a vengeance.

"Don't break anything, Maudie," said Claude.

"Just hush up," she said.

"Claude," said Dolan, "what the hell's going on around

144

here?"

Claude leaned his chair back on two legs and rocked. He crossed his left arm over his belly and rubbed his chin with his right hand.

"You know," he said, "a bunch of Brody's deputies has been killed here lately."

"Yeah," said Dolan. "That's another thing. I forgot to mention that. Five of them."

"At least," said Claude. "You're right, Alfie. There is something going on here that we don't know about."

Maude came stomping back over to the table. She leaned forward, and put her hands down on the tabletop, and gave both men a hard look.

"And when did it all start?" she said. "Use your thick skulls for something besides holding your ears apart."

"Well, let's see," said Claude. "It was just a couple of days before the celebration started. Yeah. They found them two deputies out on the road north of town."

"It was right after our three friends came to town," said Maude. "Robert D. Wade and Pawnee and Trish. That's when it started."

"They did kill two deputies over in the Tanglefoot," said Dolan, "but everyone said that was just a misunderstanding. It wasn't their fault."

"Them three came to town," said Maude. "Then deputies start getting killed. They hire on with Brody. Brody and McDowell has a falling out. McDowell disappears. Mrs. Brody runs off with Wade and them. Brody's searching high and low and calling it a kidnapping. Put it together."

Dolan stared stupidly at Maude.

"What are you getting at?" asked Claude.

Maude sat down and scooted her chair up close to the table. She looked toward the door, as if to make sure that no one was about to come in, and then she spoke in a low, confidential, almost conspiratorial voice.

"They came after Brody," she said.

"Who?" said Claude.

"Pawnee and Robert D. and Trish. That's why they came to town, and that's what's been going on."

145

"But why?" asked Claude.

"I don't know why," said Maude, "but I know it's true."

"Wait a minute," said Claude. "Now I think about it, the first day they come in here they bought a copy of that damn book, the one that McDowell wrote about Brody, and they asked me about the killing, about Bobby Madison. Maybe they knowed Madison and they're after Brody because of that."

Maude shrugged. "That could be the reason," she said.

"So what you're saying," said Dolan, "is that them three come to town to get Brody because he killed Bobby Madison, and they're the ones who killed all those deputies and caused all this other stuff to happen. Is that right?"

"Who did Susan Brody ride out of town with?" asked Maude. "Who is Brody chasing after so hard right now?"

"By God," said Dolan. "But just them three? Two men and a girl against Brody and his bunch?"

"We've got a whole town full of people here," said Claude, "and no one's had the guts to try that."

"That's just it," said Maude, shooting an accusing look at the two men. "No one's had the guts."

The three sat in silence for several minutes, no one thinking of anything further to say on the subject at hand, yet no one wanting to call an end to the discussion, either. Finally, Dolan spoke.

"So what do we do?" he asked.

It was a significant question. It was the first suggestion that someone should do something, that they should take some kind of action.

"What can we do?" asked Claude. "We can't attack Brody and his deputies, can we?"

"We can be ready," said Dolan. "That's what we can do. O'Rourke and them are going to do something. We can just be ready for it when it happens, and then we can jump in and help. They might have their reasons for going after Brody. Bobby Madison maybe. Whatever. But when it comes to freeing this town from Brody's rule . . . well, that's our business, ain't it?"

"It's our town," said Maude. "It's our business."

"That means it's our fight," said Dolan, "and I never did like to let anyone else do my fighting for me."

"What exactly do we do?" questioned Claude.

"You got a gun?" Dolan asked.

"Well, yeah. Sure."

"Keep it clean and loaded and handy," said Dolan, "and just keep your eyes and ears open. Be ready."

Brody sat in his favorite chair with his guns in his lap, a glass of brandy in his hand, and General at his feet. There were deputies outside the house. Still, he was afraid. And he was angry.

Just the other day, coming back to Drago from the capitol, he had thought that he was sitting on top of the world. He had money in the bank, and he practically owned a town. He had the grudging respect of everyone around him, and he had a wife to do his every bidding. She had to. She knew what was good for her if she didn't. And he had a promising political future. At least he had thought that he did. He had come back to town feeling great, smug even. Big shots from the capitol were coming for Drago's Birthday Celebration, and the whole theme of the celebration would be the heroism of Phil Brody. He had even dared to dream that it could all lead him eventually to Washington, yes, to the White House. He was a big man, and he had even bigger plans and dreams and schemes.

He had come back to Drago feeling great, and the first news he had received was that three of his deputies—not *just* three, the top three—had been murdered. No one knew anything about it. No one had any idea who had done the deed. And he had been waiting for the arrival of four more top guns, and soon it had become evident that they were not coming. They, too, had most likely been killed by the same perpetrators. Two more deputies had been killed, practically under his nose, and then he had begun receiving threatening letters. His organization had been temporarily infiltrated by the enemy—that damned Robert D. Wade and his partner, the half-breed—and before Brody had been able to figure out their scheme, Susan had run away with them.

"Damn," he shouted, and he threw his glass across the room, smashing it against the far wall. "Bitch. The bitch. Goddamned bitch."

General jumped up and whimpered.

"Shut up, General," said Brody. "Lay down."

General gave one last feeble whimper and flattened himself on the floor again. Brody got up and walked to the liquor cabinet for a fresh glass, then returned to his chair and poured it full of brandy. He sat back down. He was unsteady on his feet, and his head was beginning to feel a little light. He missed Susan. He wished that she were home. He didn't like being alone. Of course, he knew that if Susan came walking through the door at that very moment, he would beat her to within an inch of her life. He would make her scream, make her beg him to just go on and finish the job, to kill her and have done with it. And he would not. He would stop before it got that far, because he needed her around. He wondered where she had gone, where Robert D. Wade had taken her, and then he wondered if they were lovers. He tried to picture in his mind Robert D. Wade and Susan naked, together, doing all kinds of strange and exotic things, and it made him more furious than before.

He wanted someone to talk to about these things, but there was no one. He used to talk to Susan — some. Really, he just *told* Susan things. He had never really *talked* to her, not in years. The only person he had actually been able to talk to recently had been McDowell. Suddenly, Brody missed the newspaperman terribly. He wanted to sit down with McDowell and talk, just talk. No one else was intelligent enough to understand his conversation. He felt another violent urge boiling up inside him, but he held it back. He did not throw another glass, and he did not shout out again. Instead, he cursed McDowell silently and bitterly. The man had betrayed him and thereby brought about his own demise, but Brody realized that he missed McDowell, missed him painfully, missed him perhaps even more than he missed Susan. Yes, more. There were other women. There were several down at the Tanglefoot. He could go down there and not feel so lonely, but he was afraid to go out.

Somewhere out there, Robert D. Wade waited. Pawnee O'Rourke lurked somewhere out there, too. And the girl, Patricia Madison, wore a six-gun, and she probably wanted to kill Brody even more than all the rest.

"Where the hell are they?" he shouted aloud. "Where?"

He tossed down his brandy and got up from the chair. Then he walked to the front door and opened it.

"Who's out there?" he called. "Jones?"

"Yes, sir," said Jones. "Me and Harper. We're right here."

"Jones, I want you to make a quick run down to the Tanglefoot. Get Jonilla and bring her up here to me. Hurry up about it, 'cause I need you to be here on guard."

"Yes, sir," said Jones. "I'll get her right back up here."

As Brody slammed the door he heard Jones's footsteps on the porch. A moment later he heard the sound of a horse riding away from the house. He poured himself another brandy and sat down to wait. He needed some company, needed it bad, and Jonilla would have to do. Brody thought about the young whore, remembered her round, firm young body, recalled the way her pretty face twisted and her voice squealed when he hurt her. Jonilla would do nicely. She was stupid, but he didn't want to talk to her, anyway. He'd have to find somebody else to talk to, maybe someone from the capitol. Maybe he could locate a new editor for the newspaper. He would have to look in the cities, maybe back east. It wasn't long before he heard Jones's horse returning, and then he heard the footsteps on the porch. He went to the door and opened it just as Jonilla was walking up. He smiled a broad, leering smile.

"Come in, little darling," he said.

"Hi, Phil," said Jonilla. She swept into the big living room, and Brody slammed the door behind her. "Are you lonesome tonight?"

"Not anymore," he said, and he grabbed her and pulled her to him, mashing his open lips against her mouth.

"Come here," he said, and he led her to his favorite chair, where he sat down and then pulled her onto his lap. He reached over to the table and picked up his empty glass.

"Fill this up for me," he said.

Out front, Jones paced nervously from one end of the porch to the other and back. Harper sat in a straight chair, pushed back against the wall.

"I guess the boss is going to have a grand old time tonight," said Harper.

"Yeah," said Jones. "I guess so."

"She probably won't like it so much, though," said Harper.

"Yeah. He likes to hurt them, don't he? I don't too much cotton to that."

"It ain't none of your business," said Harper, "nor mine. You reckon that Wade and his bunch will come up here?"

"I don't know," said Jones. "I don't think they're that dumb, do you? I mean, they'd have us to get past, and even if they could take all of us, then Brody's inside the house. He could take pot shots at them out here, and there wouldn't be much they could do. If they managed to get inside, then they'd have that damned dog to worry about. I wouldn't try to attack this house. Not with just two men. No way."

"It would be kind of like committing suicide," said Harper. "You see anything out there?"

"Not a goddamned thing. You got a smoke?"

"Sure," said Harper. "Here."

He handed Jones a small sack, and the two of them rolled cigarettes and lit them. They sat in silence for a moment, smoking.

"One thing's for sure," said Jones.

"What's that?"

"One way or another, there's going to be a showdown. One way or another."

Chapter 18

Robert D. settled into his saddle and turned his mount toward the trail that led back down the hill.

"I won't be long," he said.

"I ought to ride along behind you and cover your backside," said Pawnee. "Just in case."

"You stay here with the women," said Robert D. "Just in case."

"Well, all right then. How about if I perch myself up there on that goat tower?"

"That'd be okay."

Robert D. started down the hill, and Pawnee went back to the corral after his pony.

"Be careful," said Susan, calling out after Robert D. Standing in the doorway, leaning against the frame, Trish scowled. Robert D. had sensed that Trish was irritated about something, but he had decided it was just her impatience. They had made a long trip to Drago for the purpose of avenging Bobby's murder. Then they had discovered the way in which Bobby's grave was being exploited and had determined to move the remains back to the old home place. Not only hadn't they accomplished either purpose, but they had been run out of town and were hiding at a goat camp in the hills. Well, Robert D. had a plan. It should work, and when it was all over with, Trish would he back to normal once again. She would be all right. He rode across the flat between the last two hills—the first two going down—and then he started the descent that led between the two big outcroppings of rock. The boulder that Pawnee had called the goat tower was just to his right. He rode on down the trail a ways and looked back over his shoulder. His feeling about his plan was reinforced. It was a perfect spot. He rode on down the hill and followed the trail through the mesquite thicket. As he urged his mount down into the river water, he realized that he had the same feeling he had felt many times during the war, just prior to a battle. Once again he was a commander, and he was planning a slaughter. There was a difference, though. The slaughter of the war had seemed senseless. Even thinking back on it didn't change anything. It still seemed meaningless and without purpose. He didn't know why he had killed all those men during the war, men he had not even known, could not have had any reason to kill. But this Brody cried out for killing. This battle would make sense. It would have meaning and purpose, and when it was over and done, if he survived, Robert D. would not feel empty inside. He would feel a sense of accomplishment. He rode out of the water and began the last leg of the trail back to Van Tuyl's store and home. The last piece of his plan was about to be put into play.

Van Tuyl had heard the sound of the approaching horse and was outside to meet Robert D. as he rode up.

"I didn't expect to see you so soon," he said. "What's up?"

"You still want to help?" asked Robert D.

"Damn right," said Dutch.

"I want you to go into town to see Brody. Tell him you heard he was looking for me—me and my partners. Say that we came by here for supplies and we had his wife with us. Then tell him that you tailed us long enough to find out where we were going. Tell him where we're at, but convince him that we feel safe. We don't think anyone can find us up there. We won't be looking for him."

"You want him to come after you," said Dutch.

"I can set a perfect trap on that trail," said Robert D. "Is there any other way up there?"

"Not one that would take him there in less than a week," said Dutch. "He'll have to come right up that trail."

"Good. Tell him what I said. Tell him you're just being a good citizen."

"Just let me tell Lisa," said Dutch, "and I'll be on my way."

Trish was picking up her pallet from the floor when Susan walked back into the cabin. Trish jerked up the blanket and turned her back on the other woman. Susan walked over to the cot and sat on its edge.

"If I had known that you didn't need that cot," said Trish, "I wouldn't have slept on the floor last night."

The silence was thick and tense for a long moment.

"You can have the cot," said Susan.

"I don't need it," Trish snapped back. Her voice was icy cold.

"Trish," said Susan, "don't hate me because of my husband. I made the biggest mistake of my life when I married Phil Brody, but I didn't know what he was like. My life with Phil has been one long misery. It's been a prison and a torture chamber. I want to see him dead just as much as you do, probably more. You saw what he did to me. Or are you one of those people who think that some women enjoy this sort of thing? Believe me, I don't. I'd kill him myself if I had the chance."

Trish thought that Susan had probably had plenty of chances. Either she didn't really want to kill Brody, or she was a coward. Probably the latter. No. She didn't think that Susan enjoyed her life with her husband, not after what Brody had done to her. Trish did believe Susan about all that, but that wasn't what was bothering her.

"You're just using Uncle Bob," she said. "And I don't like that."

Susan stood up in surprise.

"Is that it?" she said. "You—Trish, I love Robert D. Can't you understand that? And I believe that he loves me. You

153

can't hold that against me?"

Trish stared long and hard at Susan. Her chest was heaving with her short, quick breaths, and she could feel her increased heartbeat pounding furiously.

"Susan," she said, "you're no good. I don't know what you're up to, but I know this. If Uncle Bob is fool enough to marry you, he'll just wind up the way you did with Brody. After it's too late, he'll find out that he made a big mistake. And I'll do whatever I can to keep him from making that mistake."

She turned to walk out of the house, but Susan stopped her.

"Trish," she said, and her voice was suddenly hard and threatening, "if you come between us, you're the one who will be cut out of Robert D.'s life, not me."

Trish stormed out of the house with the awful feeling that Susan was probably right. Pawnee was just coming around the corner with his pony saddled. She almost ran into him.

"Whoa there," he said.

"I'm sorry."

"I'm just fixing to ride down the trail as far as that there goat tower," he said. "Watch over things from up there. Want to go along?"

"Yeah," she said. "I'll get my horse."

"Here," said Pawnee, handing her the reins to his pony. "I'll fetch him."

Pawnee saddled Trish's horse and they rode in silence down the trail until they came to the big rock. The scout found a way back around it. They left their horses there at the base of the rock and climbed to the top.

"This is even better than I thought," said Pawnee. "You can see pert' near to the mesquite."

"Yeah," said Trish. She was still surly. Pawnee looked at her. Once again he felt the strong desire to put his arms around her and offer her comfort. Perhaps he felt more than that, but he wouldn't allow himself to think those kinds of thoughts about Trish. He turned his back on her and sat down on the rock, staring off down the trail.

"Trish," he said without turning his head to look at her.

154

"What?"

"It probably ain't none of my business. I didn't mean to, but I heard some of that talk back there. Between you and Miz Brody."

"The bitch," said Trish.

"Back off, Trish," said Pawnee. "She's right. You'll just run them together."

"Pawnee, I just can't stand the thought of her with Uncle Bob. She went to him last night, did you know that?"

"I know. But it ain't none of my business, just like it ain't yours."

"But, Pawnee—"

"Trish," said Pawnee, surprised at the sharpness in his own voice, "if you're right about that woman, Robert D. will figure it all out for himself."

Trish walked to the back edge of the big boulder. She was silent for a moment. Her back was turned to Pawnee. He sat at the other edge, his back still to her. Finally, Trish broke the silence.

"I wish Brody had beat her to death," she said.

Pawnee put a palm to his forehead and groaned. Then he stood up and walked over to Trish. She still had her back to him.

"I don't like to see you like this," he said. "Brody's one thing, because of what he done to your brother. I can understand that. But you're about ate up with hate, Trish, and I— I can't hardly stand it."

Trish turned suddenly and threw her arms around Pawnee, lying her head against his shoulder. Slowly, reluctantly, he put his arms around her. This should be a brotherly embrace, he told himself, and he patted her gently on the back.

"I'm sorry," she said. "I didn't mean it. I don't want her dead. I just don't want Uncle Bob to get hurt."

"I know, baby," he said. "Everything's going to be all right."

When Brody first woke up that morning, he thought it

was Susan there beside him. Then the events of the previous evening slowly came back to him. Susan was gone. The bitch. She had run off with Robert D. Wade. And before he had gone to bed, Brody had sent one of the deputies down to the Tanglefoot to bring back Jonilla, his favorite whore. Brody sat up on the edge of the bed and moaned. He stood up and stretched, found his trousers, and pulled them on. He looked back at Jonilla. She was still asleep, lying there under one thin sheet. He reached across the bed, took hold of the sheet, and jerked it off her in one motion.

"Wake up," he said.

Jonilla whimpered sleepily and stirred a bit, then snuggled back down into the pillow. Her eyes had never opened. Brody walked around the bed, keeping his eyes on her naked body. When he got to the other side, he gave her a vicious slap on the bare buttocks. She screamed and sat up.

"Get up," said Brody. "Fix me some coffee."

Jonilla had spent nights with Brody before, and she knew better than to cross him. She got up and picked up her dress from the floor. Brody opened a closet door and found one of Susan's robes. He threw it across the room at Jonilla.

"Here," he said. "Use this."

She pulled on the robe and headed for the kitchen. Back behind his door, General barked furiously. It sent a chill up Jonilla's spine. Brody pulled on his boots and slipped on a shirt. Then he heard a pounding at the door. General barked again.

"Shut up, General," Brody shouted as he headed for the door. Jones was there on the porch. "What is it?" asked Brody.

"Rider coming, boss," said Jones. "You said to let you know."

Brody stepped out onto the porch with Jones. Harper was there, too, holding his shotgun and watching the approaching rider.

"It looks like that damn Dutchman," said Jones.

"What the hell does he want?" asked Brody. "Bring that chair over here."

Jones dragged over the chair that stood on the porch and

Brody sat down in it, a deputy standing on either side. Soon Dutch Van Tuyl rode up and stopped there by the porch. He stayed in the saddle as he talked.

"Sheriff Brody," he said.

"Yeah," said Brody.

"I got some information for you."

"What kind of information?"

"Well," said Dutch, "I heard you was looking for that man Wade and his partners."

"Well," said Brody, "go on."

"They stopped by my place last night. You know, Van Tuyl's out on the south road."

"All of them?" asked Brody.

"Wade, O'Rourke, and that girl — Trish, they called her," said Dutch.

"That all?" said Brody.

"I'm sorry to have to tell you this, Sheriff," said Dutch, "but your wife was with them, too."

Brody's face turned red, but he managed to restrain his anger. He stood up and walked to the opposite end of the porch and stared out across the prairie for at least a minute. Dutch wondered if he had been dismissed. Then Brody turned and walked back to his chair. This time, however, he stood behind it. He didn't speak. He just looked at Dutch.

"They stopped in for supplies," said Dutch. "Like trail supplies, you know? I was afraid to refuse them service. I gave them what they wanted and they rode on."

"Which direction?" asked Brody.

"I figured you'd want to know," said Dutch, "so I give them a little head start, and then I followed them. They turned east, went across the river and rode up the trail to the goatman's cabin. That's where they camped. Big as you please. They act like they're the only ones around who know the place is out there. I watched them for a while. They didn't even post no guards."

"Where's this goatman's place?" asked Brody.

"I know where it is, boss," said Jones. "I'd forgot all about it 'til just now. The old man died a few months ago."

"You think they're still out there?" asked Brody, looking

back toward Dutch.

"I'd bet on it," said Dutch. "It looked to me like they'd set up permanent housekeeping."

"All right," said Brody. "You can go. Go on."

Dutch turned his horse and headed back toward Drago. Brody turned to Jones. He took hold of the deputy's shirt-front and pulled him up close.

"Get all the boys together," he said. "Get the horses. Mine, too. Get rid of those damn shotguns, and arm every man with two revolvers and a rifle. Pack plenty of ammunition. Gather up right here. Fast."

Chapter 19

Robert D. waited at the Van Tuyl store until Dutch returned from his trip into Drago to see Brody. He was standing in front of the store when Dutch rode up.

"How'd it go?" he asked.

"Brody was giving orders before I even rode off," said Dutch. "He was arming everybody to the teeth. They'll be along any minute."

"Good," said Robert D. "I'd best get back up the hill."

"I'm coming with you," said Dutch.

Robert D. started to protest, but then he thought of the vulnerable position Dutch and Lisa would be in out there on the road. Probably Brody was not suspicious of the Van Tuyls, but just in case he was, they would be safer up at the cabin.

"That's a good idea," he said. "But bring Lisa with you. You don't want her down here alone."

Dutch went inside after his wife and returned in just a couple of minutes. The Van Tuyls had only the one saddle horse, so they had to ride double. Before coming out of his store, Dutch had grabbed up extra weapons and ammunition. So far there was no sign of Brody and his posse on the road, but Robert D. had Dutch ride ahead anyhow. If the posse did come up on them, he would be able to protect them from the rear.

* * *

The deputies were gathered outside Brody's big blue house, all mounted. A saddled horse waited for Brody. Each deputy carried two revolvers and had a rifle in a saddle scabbard. There was a loaded rifle in the scabbard attached to Brody's saddle as well. Saddlebags on each horse were loaded with extra ammunition. At last Brody stepped out onto the porch. He had washed and shaved, and he was dressed in a clean black three-piece suit. The vest was buttoned up over a fresh white silk shirt. A black tie was knotted around the collar. Brody's badge was pinned to the left breast of the black coat. It had been polished and was shining against the black background. Around his waist a black leather belt was strapped, and it held two black leather holsters that were tied down to Brody's thighs. Each holster contained a Smith and Wesson .45. Brody's suit trousers were tucked into high-top black leather boots that had a gleaming shine, and on his head he wore a black wide-brimmed hat with a low, flat crown. His dark brown mustache had been freshly waxed and was turned up into a bristling handlebar. He stopped and postured on the porch, his thumbs hooked in his belt, and surveyed his posse. Finally, he spoke.

"Men," he said, "have every piece fully loaded. These are dangerous criminals we're going after. Take no chances and give no quarter. Shoot to kill. And that order includes the woman. She's as deadly a gunfighter as the men. In fact, I have recently discovered that her full name is Patricia Madison. She's the sister of Bobby Madison, and she's as handy and quick with her guns as he was. There's three of them, and they're holding a hostage. They've got Mrs. Brody. Try not to hit her, but don't let her stop you from doing your duty. Mr. Jones, you know where we're going, so you take the lead. Let's ride, men."

Brody stepped from the porch into the saddle. The posse wheeled about and headed south, riding through Drago on the main street and continuing out the south road. At the far end of the street a small band had gathered and the musicians were busily tuning their instruments in preparation for a parade. Children ran along the street in the wake of the posse, shouting and waving, until they could no longer keep up and had gotten

160

tired of eating the dust from the horses' hooves. It was a grand military-looking posse, and except for the fact that it was going in the wrong direction and too fast, it might have been the beginning of the parade. The governor was standing on the sidewalk beside Maximillian Sweet.

"What's going on around here, Mr. Sweet?" he asked.

"I'm not sure, your honor . . . uh . . . your . . . uh . . . governor, sir," said Sweet. "I think there are some outlaws loose or something like that. I'm sure it's an emergency, or else Mr. Brody—that is, Sheriff Brody—would be here for the celebration."

"I'm sure," said the governor.

Jones led the posse out the south road until they were within a half mile of Van Tuyl's store. Then he turned east. They rode to the river and crossed it. Then they were in the thicket, and the path through the mesquite trees was narrow. From there on it would be single-file riding. Brody let Harper follow Jones, then had Sand fall in line. Brody rode next, and the other three took up the rear. That put three ahead and three behind Brody, and he felt well protected.

Pawnee heard before he saw. He stood up on the rock and chambered a shell in the Winchester. Then Dutch and Lisa appeared on the trail below, riding double. Close behind them came Robert D. Pawnee waved the Winchester in the air, and Robert D. lifted a hand in response. He rode a little closer before he yelled up at Pawnee.

"Stay there," he called. "Brody and his bunch will be coming along."

They rode on to the goatman's cabin and dismounted. Trish and Susan were standing outside waiting to meet them. Robert D. could read the question on their faces.

"Brody's coming along," he said. "We'll be ready for them."

"How many are coming?" asked Trish.

"All seven," said Robert D. "Dutch, you can take these horses around back. And saddle up three more just in case we need them in a hurry. Dump all those guns you brought inside on the table first."

161

Dutch put the guns inside, then went around back with the horses. Robert D. and the three women were in the house. Robert D. stuffed his pockets with ammunition.

"I'm going down there with Pawnee," he said. "I want the rest of you to stay here."

"I can shoot as well as you can," said Trish, "and I want Brody worse than you do."

"And he or some of his men might break through and come up here. I want you here. You and Dutch. That trail's so narrow, they can only come up single file. Two of us can cover it good enough. But what if they know a way around that we don't know about? What if they pick one of us off the rock — or both — and get past us?"

Trish couldn't think of an argument, so she just sulked in silence. Robert D. usually knew what was best. That didn't mean she always liked it. Robert D. turned to the two other women.

"Can you handle a gun?" he asked.

"If I have to," said Susan.

"I can," said Lisa.

"I hope you don't have to, but you never know," said Robert D. "There's plenty of them here. Just be ready for anything."

He started out the door, and Susan hurried after him, catching him just as he stepped outside.

"Robert D." she said, reaching around his neck and pulling his head down to hers for a kiss, "be careful. I don't want to lose you."

Just inside the cabin, Trish clenched her teeth and furrowed her brow. Lisa noticed and thought that she understood. Robert D. broke loose from the embrace and walked around behind the cabin. Taking his horse by the reins, he paused to speak with Dutch.

"I'm going down to join Pawnee and wait for Brody there," he said. "We'll probably stop them there. It's a good spot for an ambush. But you never know how these things will turn out. You stay here with the women in case we fail."

He put a foot in a stirrup and swung up into the saddle.

* * *

As the trail up into the hills narrowed and the walls became steeper on either side, Brody began to get nervous. Those outlaw bastards could lay an ambush along here just about anywhere, he thought. Then he considered the Dutchman. He had wondered briefly why the Dutchman, who had never before been particularly cooperative with the sheriff's office, had come to him with news of Wade and his band. Then he had dismissed the thought. He had wanted to get Wade and the others so badly that he had made quick and easy excuses for the Dutchman. But riding along this trail, watching the rocks to each side rise higher and higher, feeling the walls closing in, the trail narrowing almost with each step, the sheriff wondered if the Dutchman might not be involved in a conspiracy with Wade, a conspiracy to lay a trap for him. Beads of sweat appeared on Brody's forehead. He looked up the trail with a nervous eye, and he pulled back on his reins. He held up a hand to indicate to those behind him to halt, and he gestured for them to keep quiet. Directly ahead of him, Sand turned in his saddle to see what was going on. Brody waved at him to continue on. He sat there in his saddle for a moment, watching Sand disappear around a curve in the narrow trail. Then he gestured again to the riders behind him, this time to turn their horses around on the trail. He turned his own with some difficulty. The trail was just wide enough at that point to allow the turning. When the riders had all reversed their directions, they waited for further instructions from their boss. Brody had already ridden right up against Moss's mount.

"Go on," he said in a harsh whisper. "Go on."

Puzzled, Moss, Watts, and Collins started back down the trail, Brody right behind and hurrying them along. As he got farther away from the ambush he was envisioning and the three deputies he had just betrayed, he also got bolder. His harshly whispered urgings became louder commands.

"Hurry it along there," he said. "Goddamn it. Move on."

As he rode he kept looking nervously back over his shoulder, and it was with a great sense of relief that Brody rode down out of the foothills and into the mesquite thicket. Riding through the stunted, thorny trees on the narrow trail, he even stopped nagging at his deputies. He rode with a certain amount of ease. If those three he had sent on ahead were worth a damn, he thought, they would kill Wade and the others anyway. Coming out of the thicket, Brody, confident and arrogant once more, moved out ahead of the deputies. As they rode into the water to cross the river, they heard the first shots in the distance behind them.

"Boss?" said Collins.

Brody continued riding straight ahead.

"They're into it back there," said Collins.

Brody rode on, looking straight ahead. Watts and Moss followed him, although a bit reluctantly. Collins had stopped midstream. His horse was prancing uncertainly in the water. Both horse and rider seemed undecided as to which way to go. Brody rode out of the water on the other side. Only then did he turn back to answer Collins.

"Come on," he shouted. "I know what the hell I'm doing. That's why I'm in charge here."

Collins looked back one more time. Another gunshot sounded in the distance. He followed his boss on across the river.

"Now listen to me," said Brody. "Them up in the hills were not expecting us to attack. There's only two men up there and one woman. Jones and Harper and Sand can handle that with no problem. They don't need us along. I have reason to believe that the Dutchman and his wife are part of the gang, and that's why we've come back down here. We're going to attack both of their strongholds at the same time by surprise."

He pulled one of his revolvers out and held it up ready. Then he turned his horse toward the Van Tuyl store.

"All right, men," he shouted, "let's go."

Brody rode as if he were leading a cavalry attack. With his pistol held ready, he charged full speed the whole distance across the flat prairie between the river and the store. It was a ludicrous attack. Arriving at the store, Brody and his three deputies simply reined in and stopped. They sat there, wondering what to do next. Finally, Brody blurted out another command.

"Go inside and drag them out here," he said.

As the three deputies dismounted and charged through the

164

front door, Brody backed his horse away to a safer distance to wait. The only gunshots he heard were faint, off in the distance, somewhere up in the hills he had left far behind. Soon the deputies came back outside.

"Ain't no one in there," said Watts.

A look of confusion passed quickly over Brody's face. Then he re-furrowed his brow and twisted his features back into a grim and stern commanding expression.

"Burn it," he said.

The three deputies looked around for some dry brush, something with which to start a fire. They saw nothing. They looked at each other and at Brody. Watts felt his shirt pockets and looked at Moss.

"You got any matches?" he asked.

Moss patted his own pockets and shrugged.

"I don't smoke," he said.

Brody took a cigar out of his breast pocket and stuck it in his mouth. He reached back into the pocket for a match. None were there. He reached into another pocket, then felt all his remaining pockets. He had no matches. Finally, Collins saved the day for the would-be arsonists.

"I bet they got some in the store," he said, and he led the deputies back inside. After a few minutes of searching shelves, Moss found the matches.

"Here they are," he said. He took a box off the shelf and tossed it to Collins. Watts had come over to his side, and he handed him one. Finally, he picked up a third box for himself. Collins headed for the living quarters in the back. There were curtains on the windows. He struck a match and set each curtain ablaze, then he hurried back out into the store. Watts had found some papers behind the counter and had wadded them up into a pile on the floor beneath. He struck a match and lit the pile. Still at the shelf with the matches, Moss was holding a flame to a matchbox on the bottom of the stack. Soon there was a burst of flame, as if someone had struck a giant match. Moss jumped back in fright.

"Let's get out of here," he said.

They ran back out the front door and mounted up, and as the flames began to lick their way through the building, the four riders moved back to a safe and comfortable distance and watched. Brody still held his unlit cigar between his lips.

"Anybody got a match?" he asked.

Chapter 20

The rock across the path from Pawnee's goat tower was not as high as was the other, but it still afforded a good view of the trail below and good cover. Robert D. left his horse with Pawnee's behind the big rock, then crossed the trail and climbed up on top of the smaller one. The two seasoned gunfighters had been together through so many scraps that they hardly needed words to communicate. In some situations they almost knew beforehand what the other would do, so that even looks and gestures became superfluous. When they heard the approaching hoofbeats on the path below, they exchanged glances. That was all. Then they waited. Soon Jones came riding into view. Still they waited. Then came Harper. Robert D. and Pawnee stood up almost together, rifles in hand, aimed at the two men below.

"Hold it right there," said Robert D.

The riders stopped and looked up.

"If you'll throw down your hardware and keep riding ahead slow and easy, you can live," said Robert D.

Harper glanced around. He could tell that as long as he sat in the saddle, the two outlaws had good, clean shots at him, but if he could manage to dismount before they could get off a shot, the steep walls would afford him some cover. He suddenly lunged off the saddle to his left, dropping to the ground with a hard thud and rolling himself up snug against the rocks. Pawnee's shot was an instant too late. Jones grabbed for his six-gun while throwing up his left leg and tossing himself backward and to the right. He fired as he fell, his bullet kicking up shards of rock at Pawnee's feet. The two riderless horses ran ahead on the path. Robert D. turned and slid down the back side of the boulder on which he had been perched. Pawnee inched out farther toward the front edge of his goat tower. As he peered over the edge, looking almost straight down, he and Jones saw each other at once, and they fired almost simultaneously. The deputy's bullet tore a hole in the edge of Pawnee's left ear, but the scout's rifle slug found its mark near the center high on Jones's forehead. Because of the steep angle from which it had been fired, it exited between the deputy's shoulder blades in back. Jones gave one convulsive jerk of his whole body, then collapsed into a lifeless lump.

Pawnee ducked quickly back out of sight, blood running down his neck from the nick in his ear.

"Damn," he said. The ear felt as if it had been stung by a very large bee. Two shots from Harper's revolver ricocheted off the boulder in front of him as he moved back. Where Robert D. had landed on the ground, two boulders were nestled together, leaving a low crawl space between them, like a natural tunnel, which led to the path. Robert D. laid aside his rifle, pulled out his revolver, and ducked low. He started to inch his way through the tunnel. Out on the trail, Harper turned around and looked behind him. He could see Sand back there, still mounted. The other deputy had not yet come into Pawnee or Robert D.'s view. Sand looked at Harper, who held up two fingers, then pointed at the two rocks that towered over his cringing figure. Sand nodded his understanding, slipped the rifle out of its scabbard, and slowly dismounted. He steadied his frightened horse, trying to decide what his move should be. To his left was a narrow passageway between two boulders. It looked as if he could just squeeze through, but it might lead him around behind the tall boulder up ahead, one of the two at which Harper had pointed. He stood up as tall as he could in an attempt to squeeze himself thin, then began inching his way through.

Meanwhile Harper had begun moving uphill, still in a sitting position with his back pressed against the wall. Pawnee was somewhere up above him. He knew that. He had not heard anything from Robert D. since falling from his horse, but he was facing Wade's side of the path. He didn't like that. He couldn't see the man directly above to get off a shot. He looked up and down the path. No one moved. He heard no sound. Slowly, he raised up on his feet and threw himself across the path. He huddled, breathless, against the rock wall there, expecting shots to follow him. None did. He waited another thirty seconds, then resumed his sidling motion uphill.

Robert D. was practically on his belly in the rat hole through which he crawled. Up ahead he could see the light that was his goal. He would emerge out on the trail. He reached out in front of himself with both arms, then lifted and pulled with his elbows. It was slow but steady progress. Then something moved across the hole up ahead, and Robert D.'s tunnel darkened: It had to be somebody. He raised his gun hand slightly off the ground. His arm was stretched out full length before him. He thumbed back the hammer and fired. Out in the trail, Harper shouted out once in pain and surprise as the bullet smashed through spinal cord just below the rib cage. Robert D. crawled on ahead in darkness. When he finally reached the end of the tunnel, he pushed the body away, then waited. There was no sound. Nothing. He crawled on out into the trail and stood up. He looked both ways. Still he saw nothing. He looked up toward Pawnee's rock.

"Pawnee," he said in a loud whisper. "Down here."

Pawnee appeared at the edge of the boulder and looked down.

"We got two of them," said Robert D. "You see the others anywhere?"

Pawnee looked down the trail and saw no one. He stood up slowly. Still the trail was empty. He stretched his neck.

"I see a third horse," he said. "I don't see his rider."

"I'm coming around," said Robert D. and he ran behind the big boulder. He was just starting to climb up to join Pawnee when Sand stepped out in the open behind him, aiming his rifle between Robert D.'s shoulder blades. Pawnee loomed up on top of the rock and fired a quick shot over Robert D.'s head and into Sand's chest. The deputy took a step backward. His rifle barrel drooped, as if it had suddenly become heavy. He tried to raise it up again to get off his shot before he fell. He was weaving, and blood started to trickle out of a corner of his mouth. He strained to raise the rifle, and Pawnee fired again. The second shot also hit him in the chest, and with it, he gave a jerk, staggered forward two steps, then fell over on his face. Robert D. scrambled on up the rock and stood by Pawnee.

"That's three," he said. "There should have been seven. Where the hell are the others?"

"I don't see anyone down the trail," said Pawnee. "But I do see something else."

Robert D. looked at Pawnee. He was staring off as if down the trail, but farther away. Robert D. followed his gaze. There in the distance smoke was billowing up from the horizon.

"There's nothing over there but Dutch's place," said Robert D. "I'm going to check it out."

"I'll go with you," said Pawnee.

"No. You stay here. It might be a trick to draw us out into the open, or to get us away from the women so they can attack. I'll watch myself."

Robert D. hurried down the side of the big rock and mounted his waiting horse. He made his way down the trail as fast as he could with any degree of safety. Now and then he looked up to see the smoke still rising in the sky. When he reached the thicket down below, he was able to pick up a little speed while weaving his way through on the narrow trail. Once he reached the river, he could see the flames. It was the Van Tuyl place all right. He started into the river carefully, looking all around. He could see from the tracks that there had been more than the three riders by there recently, but nowhere could he see any sign of the unaccounted-for riders. He decided that they had probably stopped to burn the store and then gone on back to town. Robert D. rode up out of the river and on across the flats. The flames were roaring. It was probably too late to save anything. He rode on closer to be sure. His horse nickered and shied, afraid of the flames. He dismounted and let the reins trail on the ground, and he walked on up closer. He stared at the leaping flames and listened to the crackle. Damn, he said to himself. Everything they own is probably in there. They didn't deserve this. He hoped that he was not responsible for Brody's vengeance on the Van Tuyls. He dropped to a squatting position and rested an arm across one knee. Fighting someone like Brody wouldn't be so bad, he mused, if it weren't for the innocent folks who got caught in the middle. Suddenly, three riders raced out from around the flames to Robert D.'s left. Each held a rifle. All three rifles were trained on Robert D. Damn, he thought, I've let them catch me off guard. They must have been hiding behind the house. Going for his revolver would have been pointless. Still in his squatting position, he raised his hands resignedly. Then Brody stepped out from the opposite side of the flaming building and swung a rifle hard, smashing the butt against the back of Robert D.'s head. Robert pitched forward on his face.

When Robert D. began to come to his senses, he was sitting up in a straight-backed chair. He felt stiff and sore, and his head was throbbing with pain. He tried to think where he was, and he gradually recalled the fight on the goat trail and then the fire at the Van Tuyl place. He had been watching the fire when . . . the deputies had appeared. Then . . . he could recall no more, no more except for a sudden stunning blow to the back of his head. That was it. Someone had hit him from behind. Brody. It must have been Brody. The three remaining deputies had all been in front of Robert D. with their rifles aimed at him. Brody had hit him. He knew it. But where was he? Robert D. tried to stand up, but he couldn't move. He wanted to put a hand to his head, to the pounding up there, but he couldn't raise his hands. He was tied. Tied to a chair. He struggled, and then he heard a vicious snarl. He opened his eyes and raised his head a little. Both of those actions took much more effort than they should. And there before him on the floor was the biggest dog he could ever recall having seen. General. General was on his belly on the hardwood floor about five feet from Robert D. The dog's front paws were extended out in front of him, and his head had been lying on the floor between them. When Robert D. had struggled, General had raised his head to snarl. Other than that, he had not moved. The monstrous cross between a bloodhound and a mastiff stared with gleaming eyes at Robert D. His lips were curled back to reveal black gums and yellow fangs, which dripped pools of frothy saliva onto the floor beneath his vise-like jaws.

Robert D. sat still. If he moved, he could see, he would be ripped to pieces by this beast. That damned Brody. Of course. He was tied up in Brody's house, probably in the same room where General was usually kept locked up when there were visitors in the house. There was nothing Robert D. could do. He was helpless, more helpless than he had ever been in his life. The next move was up to Pawnee and Trish—or up to Brody.

Robert D. heard footsteps in the next room, and then the door was opened from the other side. Brody stepped into the room. General started to go to Brody, but the sheriff stopped him with a sharp command.

"Stay, General," he said. He walked, smiling, over to Robert D. "I was beginning to wonder if you were ever going to wake up, Mr. Wade. I'm glad you did."

Robert D. glared at Brody. The sheriff was still smiling. Somewhere outside fireworks went off, and Robert D. felt as if they were going off inside his head.

"Do you know why, Mr. Wade?" asked Brody. "Do you know why I'm glad that you revived?"

Robert D. just stared at Brody. He did not answer.

"It's all right, Mr. Wade," said Brody. "You can talk to me. As long as I'm here, General won't attack. Do you know why I'm glad you came to?"

"I've got a pretty good idea," said Robert D.

"I'm going to hang you. As the grand finale of the festival. The crowd will love it. I'm having a special gallows built right at the end of the street just for the occasion."

"What am I being hanged for?" question Robert D. "Or is that asking too much?"

"Why, no. Of course not. You have every right to know why you're going to die, why you're going to hang by the neck until you are dead, dead, dead. You're going to hang for the murder

172

of nine of my deputies, that's what for. You son of a bitch."

Brody swung a savage backhand to the side of Robert D.'s head, the force of which almost overturned the chair. General came to his feet, barking and snarling.

"Sit down, General, goddamn you," said Brody. "Sit. Shut up."

The dog reluctantly sat down, then dropped back down on its belly.

"Wade," said Brody, "I'm going to move you over to the window. I'm going to put you where you can see outside."

While he talked Brody moved around behind Robert D., and he began pushing the chair across the room toward a window that faced Drago. The window was curtained. When he had the chair placed where he wanted it, Brody ripped the curtain down. Robert D. could see down near the town, carpenters working on the gallows.

"I want you to have a good view, Wade," said Brody. "A good view. When it's all done, I'm going to march you down there from here, and I'm going to put the rope around your neck — *personally.* And then I'm going to *personally* open the trap door under your feet, but there won't be any drop, Wade. You know why? Because I won't have any slack in the rope. You won't drop. Your neck won't break. No. You'll strangle. Slow. Your face will turn black and your tongue will swell up and stick out of your mouth and you'll strangle real slow. And I'll be right there the whole time — laughing."

Suddenly Brody grabbed a handful of Wade's hair and shoved forward, tilting the chair up on its two front legs and pressing Robert D.'s face against the glass windowpane.

"Look at it, Wade," he shouted. "Look at it. That's where you're going to die."

173

Chapter 21

"Trish," said Pawnee, "he wouldn't let me go with him. Said it might be a trick so someone could get by and get up here."

"You should have followed him anyway, Pawnee," said Trish, "or at least let me know what was going on."

"He's been gone too long," said Susan. "We have to do something."

They were all standing out in front of the cabin and staring out toward the smoke that was still rising in the distance.

"It's got to be our house," said Lisa. "Our house and our store. Everything we own. I have to go see."

"By the time we could get there," said Dutch, "there won't be anything left to see. Still, I would like to go have a look, just to be sure. Just to know."

"Let's go," said Trish. "All of us. Let's get the horses."

Soon they were mounted and riding down the hill. Pawnee was in the lead, with Dutch right behind him. Then Susan and Lisa followed, and Trish took up the rear. Dutch and the women saw the bodies of the three deputies for the first time as they descended the hillside. Lisa and Susan each shuddered at the sight. They rode on down the hill, through the thicket and across the river. Then they stopped. The flames were dying down. There wasn't much left to burn. It was almost over. A tear ran down Lisa's cheek, and she urged her mount forward. Dutch quickly joined her. The others let them ride ahead and followed at a short but respectful distance. Soon they all stopped again, not far from what would soon be a pile of ashes. Pawnee rode up close and dismounted. He walked around the remains of the house and store, studying the ground.

"What is it, Pawnee?" asked Trish.

"It looks to me like they got him, all right," said the scout. "I think Robert D. stood right here watching the fire, and then three of them came riding out from behind over there. Then another one came from over here, but he was on foot. Robert D. fell right here."

"Shot?" asked Dutch.

"I don't think so," said Pawnee. "For one thing, there's no blood. No. I think this guy, the one on foot, I think he hit Robert D. in the back of the head. Then they took him back to Drago."

"Brody will kill him," said Susan, "if he hasn't already."

"Let's go," said Trish.

"Where to?" asked Pawnee.

"Drago. Where else?"

"Hold on," said Pawnee grabbing her reins. "That ain't what Robert D. would do. He'd make a plan."

"And look where that got him," said Trish. "Let me go."

"All right," said Pawnee. "We'll go. But let me go ahead and look things over. Give me a head start. I'll get back to you before you get to town."

Trish sat still for a moment in the saddle, looking down at Pawnee. He was right. This was the way Robert D. would approach the problem, but her patience was nearly at an end. Brody had killed her brother, made a mockery of his burial, and now he had Robert D. He might have already killed him.

"How will you look things over in there?" asked Trish. "They'll spot you in a minute."

"I'm going around the town," said Pawnee. "Remember the first time we laid eyes on Drago? We were up on a hill looking over the north end of town. That's where I'm going."

"Go on," said Trish, "but don't waste any time. We're heading straight in."

Pawnee swung up into the saddle and kicked his pony's sides. As he raced away, Trish started riding at a much slower

175

pace down the road. Pawnee shot one glance back over his shoulder and saw the other four riding toward Drago. He would have to make real good time to get around to the other side of town, look it over, and then ride back around to intercept them. He lashed at the little pony's sides with his reins.

"Come on," he said. "Come on."

Pawnee had ridden in horse races before, and he rode the same way now. This time, though, the stakes were higher. Robert D. was not only his best friend, but he was also like a father to Pawnee. And if anything, Robert D. was even more important to Trish. In Pawnee's mind, anything that Trish wanted was important. He pressed his pony even harder. Finally, he reached the back side of the rise from which he had first viewed Drago with Trish and Robert D. He topped the rise and again looked over the town. There was the big blue house, and there outside the house were five horses. Three deputies, he thought, Brody—and Robert D. They've got him in the house. He started to turn his pony to begin the return trip when his eye caught something new in the scene. He looked again. It was a gallows under construction, and it appeared to be almost finished.

"Damn," he said, and he started to ride.

Trish called a halt to the group of riders she was leading into town. Drago was just ahead, and they would be there in another couple of minutes.

"Let's give Pawnee a little more time," she said.

"What are we going to do when we get into town?" asked Susan.

"There's only four of them left," said Trish. "Brody and three deputies. We're going in shooting."

"I can't do that," said Susan.

"Then keep out of the way."

Trish had little patience for women who were feminine. She knew, of course, that she had been raised differently, and that she shouldn't really expect other women to share her abilities and her toughness. Still she found it hard to be tolerant of their

176

softness and shyness and cowardice. Besides all that, she simply didn't like Susan. She thought of Lisa. Actually, Lisa probably would be no better off or of no more use in a fight than Susan. She turned toward Lisa.

"You can go with her," she said.

"I go with Dutch," said Lisa.

"Lisa," said Dutch, "listen to Trish. I'm going with her, but there's no need for you to go. You—"

"I'm going with you," said Lisa.

"All right," said Susan, "then I'm going along, too."

Trish started to tell Susan that she didn't want her along, that she would just get in the way, but she changed her mind. Let her come along, she thought. Maybe she'll catch a stray bullet. Who cares? Just then Pawnee appeared on the horizon. He rode up to the others, his pony puffing and blowing. Pawnee, too, was short of breath.

"It looks to me like they've got Robert D. in Brody's house. Brody and the three deputies are in there, too. Anyhow, that's how I read it"

"Let's ride," said Trish.

"Wait. There's one more thing you ought to know," said Pawnee. "They're building a gallows."

Trish sat silent in the saddle for a moment. All of a sudden she was not in such a hurry. She was thinking.

"Which one of us would attract the least attention going into town alone?" she asked.

"That's easy," said Lisa. "Me. What do you want me to do?"

"Ride into Maude's cafe. That's close to this end of town. You might be able to get in and out without attracting any real attention. Ask Maude or Claude when the hanging's set for. Then get back here and let us know."

"All right," said Lisa.

Dutch reached over and squeezed her hand.

"Be careful," he said.

"Yeah," added Trish. "If anything looks wrong to you, beat it back out here quick."

Lisa rode on toward town. She rode in at a leisurely pace in an attempt to appear to be making a casual ride into town. Pawnee studied Trish's face as she watched Lisa's figure recede.

"Trish," he said, "you want to let the rest of us in on it?"

"What?" she asked.

"What you're planning."

"I was planning an attack on Brody's house," she said, "but that was a stupid idea. I'd have done it, anyhow, and I still would if that was the only way. But if they intend to hang Uncle Bob, they'll have to bring him out of the house and walk him down to the gallows. It'll be a hell of a lot easier to take them then than it would be at the house, and the chances of Uncle Bob not getting hurt are a lot better that way, too."

Pawnee nodded his approval.

"Now you're thinking like Robert D. Wade," he said.

Trish drew the rifle out of the scabbard on her saddle and handed it to Susan.

"Here," she said. "You need something to carry even if you don't shoot it."

"Thanks," said Susan. "I'll shoot it—if I have to."

In a few minutes, Lisa came back.

"The gallows is finished," she said. "They'll be bringing Robert D. out any minute now."

"Let's go then," said Trish. They started riding, five abreast, toward Drago. Dutch took the pistol out of his belt and handed it to Lisa. They rode on steadily. Trish pulled out her own six-gun, and Pawnee hauled out his Winchester. Dutch took the rifle out of his scabbard. They rode on, faces grim and determined. This is a crazy bunch, thought Pawnee. Two of us, maybe three, can shoot a gun. They rode on, and they were at the edge of town. People on the sidewalk stared at them in wonder and curiosity. Two men and three women riding abreast down the main street, guns in hand. What could they be up to? Then Alfie Dolan appeared from somewhere. He stood on the sidewalk, a Winchester in his big hands, and as the five riders went past, he stepped out into the street to walk along behind them. Claude stepped out of Maude's Fine Food and quickly put it all together.

"Wait for me," he yelled. He ran back inside the cafe and in a minute returned with a rifle in his hands, then he fell in step behind the horses. Maude stepped out with a pistol.

"Claude," she called, "you're not going anywhere without me."

She ran until she caught up with her husband, and then she walked along beside him. Now they were eight. Two cowboys were standing on the sidewalk in front of the Tanglefoot as the strange group was passing.

"Hey," shouted one. "What the hell's going on?"

"Brody's through in Drago," answered Claude.

The cowboy looked at his buddy.

"Come on," he said, and the two cowboys ran out into the street and got in line.

Up at the blue house, Brody had just finished dressing. He went into his living room where the three deputies were lounging about.

"Just about time," he said. He went to his liquor cabinet for some brandy, and he finished the drink in two gulps. Then he went to the room in which General still stood guard over the bound Robert D. Brody entered the room, closing the door behind him.

"Stay, General," he said. He walked over to Robert D.

"It's time to hang," he said. He knelt and untied Robert D.'s feet, then stood up and untied his wrists. He unwound the ropes that held Robert D. to the straight-backed chair. Backing away quickly, he pulled out a revolver.

"All right," he said, "stand up slow and easy. You don't want to excite General here."

Robert D. stood. All his muscles tingled from the effort because he had been tied to the chair for so long.

"Now walk to the door."

Robert D. took a tentative step, and General sprang to his feet with a beastly snarl.

"General," shouted Brody "Stay. Stay. And shut up."

The dog obeyed, but obviously it was taking all his will-power to do so. He watched Robert D. hungrily, and he drooled.

"Keep going," said Brody.

Robert D. made it to the door.

"Now open it and go in the next room."

Robert D. did as he was told. The three deputies, fearful

that General might come through the open door, were up on their feet, guns in their hands. General did not come out but Robert D. did, followed by Brody. The sheriff shut the door again, closing in General, and then he tossed some ropes toward the deputies.

"Tie this bastard's hands behind him," he said.

Collins picked up the ropes and tied Wade's hands once more. Even if I could get my hands on a gun, Robert D. thought, I couldn't make my fingers work. I'm useless. No good. Brody walked up close to Robert D. and smiled.

"I want to give you something to remember me by," he said, and Brody drove a fist into Robert D.'s stomach. Robert D. doubled over from the blow, but recovered quickly and straightened up again.

"Don't worry, Sheriff Brody," he said. "I won't forget you."

"You will when you're dead," said Brody. "And that won't be long now. Get going."

He gave Robert D. a shove toward the front door. Collins was there to open it, and Brody pushed Robert D. again, this time through the door and out onto the porch. He followed Robert D. out and gave him another shove, which sent him headlong down the stairs and sprawling in the dirt.

"Get up," he snarled.

Robert D. struggled to his feet. He looked down toward the gallows at the edge of town and started walking in that direction. Brody headed for the horses.

"Come on, men," he said. "Mount up."

Robert D. kept walking, and Brody and the three deputies rode behind him. They had covered about half the distance to the gallows when Brody spotted the gang coming down the main street, led by Trish.

"Keep going, men," he said, and he turned his horse and raced back for the house.

Chapter 22

The deputies looked at each other, puzzled by Brody's sudden peculiar behavior. Robert D. was still walking. He had seen the same thing that Brody had. He was not surprised, having known all along that Trish and Pawnee would show up. But he was a little surprised at the crowd that was moving along with them. There was another crowd, too, one that had begun gathering around the gallows eagerly awaiting the forthcoming gruesome spectacle that was Sheriff Phil Brody's planned culmination of the celebration of Drago's twenty-fifth birthday. Robert D.'s footsteps quickened, and he was almost smiling as he walked on toward the new scaffold. Then Collins noticed the group led by Trish.

"Watts," he said. "Moss. Look down on Main Street."

"It's Wade's partners," said Watts. "They got a mob with them."

"They're all armed, too," said Collins.

"What do we do?" asked Moss.

"We're supposed to take this man down there to hang," said Collins. "If we fire a couple of shots down in there, they'll all run—all except them two outlaws, anyhow."

"Do we want to fight that mob?" asked Moss.

"Brody didn't," said Watts. "He took off and left us to do it."

Collins reined in his mount.

"Hold on," he said. "Let's think this over."

Robert D. kept walking. Moss and Watts stopped their horses beside Collins.

"Wait a minute, Wade," said Collins.

Robert D. continued toward the gallows.

"Wade. Hold on."

Robert D. still ignored the order, and Collins pulled out his revolver. He thumbed back the hammer and aimed at Robert D.'s back.

"Wade," he shouted, "you stop right now or I'll kill you."

Robert D. saw Pawnee raise the Winchester, and he knew that the shot was well within his partner's range. Without looking back, he flung himself to one side and landed, rolling. Pawnee pulled the trigger, and the bullet smashed Collins's left shoulder. Collins screamed in pain, dropped his revolver, and grabbed for his wounded shoulder. The crowd around the gallows began shouting and scattering in all directions. Moss, in a panic, raced his horse toward the gallows. Robert D. was right in his path, and the horse leapt over him as it hurdled forward. Robert D. struggled to his feet and ran after Moss. Watts turned a hard right and rode for the open prairie. Trish took in the situation at a glance and spurred her mount. She rode at an angle calculated to bring her between Moss and Robert D. Moss reached the gallows, which by that time was abandoned. The crowd had entirely dispersed. Trish was coming up hard behind him, and the rest of her gang, the armed and angry locals, were still down at the end of the street to the west. Moss rode around to the east end of the gallows, seeking cover. He pulled out a pistol and looked in both directions in confusion. He took aim and fired at Trish, but she dropped low in the saddle, and the bullet whizzed harmlessly over her back. She hauled back on the reins, stopping her horse right by Robert D. Leaping from the saddle, she forced the animal down on its side.

"Get down," she said, and Robert D. dropped to the ground beside the horse, sheltered from Moss's aim.

"Get me loose," he said.

"When I have time," said Trish. She fired a shot back at Moss. It missed and thudded into one of the heavy boards of the gallows stage. Moss rode around behind the gallows to get something solid between him and Trish. From down at the end of the street, Dutch fired a shot at Moss. It went wide, but it scared the deputy out from behind his cover. Again Moss looked from Trish to the gang in the street. He made a sudden, bold decision. His six-gun in his right hand, reins in the left, he spurred his horse, gave a yell, and rode hard, straight to where Trish stood with Robert D. behind the lolling horse. He fired as he rode, but the shots were wild. Trish stood her ground. Calmly, she leveled her revolver, which she held with her arm outstretched. She waited until she was sure, then she squeezed the trigger. Moss screamed and flipped backward out of the saddle. His confused horse ran on wildly.

Collins was confused, perhaps in shock. He still sat in the saddle, holding his bloody and smashed shoulder, and he rode slowly toward the street where the armed gang was gathered. He had dropped his revolver when that first shot had hit him. Another revolver hung at his left side. He seemed to have no purpose. He simply rode toward the main street. It looked as if Collins would ride right through the crowd and on through town if no one interfered. The expression on his face was blank, dazed. He was six feet from where Dutch sat on his horse, Lisa to his right and Susan to his left. Claude, Maude, the two cowboys, and other locals on foot gathered around. At first the crowd began to part, as if to let Collins ride through, and the deputy kept riding straight ahead. He rode between Dutch and Lisa, and as he passed they turned their horses to watch him. Then the picture of the flames consuming their house and store came back into Dutch's mind, and he was no longer looking at a wounded, confused man. Now he was looking at one of the uniforms of the hated deputies of Sheriff Brody. He raised his rifle and fired a shot into Collins's back. Collins gave a jerk. Lisa fired a shot into his side. One of the cowboys fired, then the other, and even when Collins's bullet-riddled body hit the dirt, they kept firing. All the hatred and fear built up over the long months under the brutal control of Brody was being taken out on the body of one dead deputy.

Pawnee was not among this crowd. When Watts had headed west across the prairie, Pawnee had given chase. Both riders were by this time well out of sight of all the rest.

A sudden, grim calm reigned over Drago. Robert D. rolled over to present his backside to Trish.

"Now?" he said.

Trish untied his hands and helped him to his feet. Then she pulled the horse back up.

"You all right?" she asked.

"I will be as soon as I get the circulation back in my arms," he said. He put an arm around her shoulders. "Good work, honey."

Trish looked over her shoulder at the blue house that loomed on the horizon. Brody's horse was there by the front porch. The granite spire stood lonely in the backyard.

"It's not over yet," she said.

"Soon," said Robert D. "Real soon."

Pawnee's pony was tired. It had just made two hard runs, and a third one so soon would be too much to ask of the faithful wretch. Pawnee ran the pony in pursuit of Watts, but he ran easy. The easy run would be good for the pony. Watts was running hard and the distance between them was increasing, but Pawnee knew that the deputy's horse would not be able to keep up that hard pace for long. He would slow down, and then the little pony with his steady pace would begin to shorten the gap between them. There was nothing out there, not for a long ways. Pawnee knew that. So catching the man was just a matter of persistence. Pawnee had ridden only about a mile out of Drago when he saw Watts's horse stumble up ahead, no more than another half mile away. Watts was thrown headlong out of the saddle and sent sprawling on the hard ground up ahead of where the pitiful horse lay.

"Horse killer," said Pawnee contemptuously. He held his pony down to an easy lope, still moving straight for Watts. The deputy scrambled to his feet and staggered backward, still stunned from the hard fall. One side of his face was raw from scraping the hard ground. Watts looked back along his trail and saw the relentless scout coming toward him, and he pulled a revolver out of its holster. Then, considering the distance, he

184

thought better of his hasty decision, shoved the six-shooter back into the holster, and ran over to the struggling horse. He pulled the rifle from the saddle holster and quickly chambered a shell. He put the rifle to his shoulder and took careful aim. Almost in one easy motion, Pawnee pulled out his Winchester, swung down out of the saddle, and gave his little pony a slap on the rump. The pony trotted off to one side, and Watts's shot went wide. Pawnee dropped down to one knee, but before he was prepared to fire, Watts had turned to run. Pawnee stood up and continued after his prey on foot. Up ahead, Watts stumbled and rolled forward into an old buffalo wallow. He scampered to his feet, then he realized the advantage of the depression he had fallen into. He dropped down on his stomach at the edge of the wallow and took aim.

Pawnee raised his Winchester and squeezed the trigger, but all he got was a dull click. He dropped the rifle and dived to his left. Watts's bullet kicked up dust just back of where Pawnee had been standing. Pawnee pulled out his right-hand revolver, but he knew that it was next to useless. The range was too great. He could see that Watts was leveling his rifle for another shot. He waited for a moment, then rolled rapidly to his right. Again, Watts's bullet hit the spot he had just left. He had moved to the left and then to the right. If Watts had any shooting savvy, he would lead his next shot a little to the left, expecting Pawnee to continue the same evasive tactic. Watts leveled his rifle for another shot, and Pawnee took another calculated pause, then rolled to his right: He was back where he had dropped his Winchester, and he had guessed right about Watts's move. The bullet hit far to his left.

Pawnee picked up his Winchester and tried to work the lever. It was jammed. He had been afraid of that. He rolled over on his back in order to present the smallest possible target to Watts, and he held the rifle across his chest while he worked to extricate the offending tilted cartridge. Watts fired again, and Pawnee heard the bullet whiz slightly above him. A small adjustment, and Watts would be on target. He kept working on the tilted cartridge.

Down in the buffalo wallow, Watts realized that Pawnee had not returned fire for some time. He figured out that something

185

must be wrong. The scout was either out of bullets or his rifle was out of order. The distance between the two men was too great for a pistol shot. He had him. He stood up to get a better shot. Even so, he thought, he could still miss. He walked closer, and he could see that the scout was working on his rifle. He took a few more steps to make absolutely sure. From this distance he couldn't possibly miss. He smiled and raised the rifle to his shoulder.

The cartridge slipped in place, and Pawnee rolled to his left, bringing the rifle to firing position out in front of him at the same time. He pulled the trigger a second after Watts pulled his. Watts's bullet hit the ground where the scout had been before the roll, but Pawnee's hit its mark. It tore right through Watts's navel. Pawnee fired again, and the second bullet smashed through Watts's chest, tearing a hole in his heart. He dropped dead on the hard prairie ground.

By the time Pawnee rode back into Drago, the crowd of angry armed citizens led by Trish had gathered in front of the Brody house. Trish and Robert D. were there in front of the crowd, and Pawnee could see that his partner was armed once again. He rode on down to join them, leaving his pony to wander at will back behind the mob. People were shouting.

"Looks like some kind of standoff," he said to Robert D.

"Yeah."

"Let's do something, Uncle Bob," said Trish.

"All right," said Robert D. "Pawnee, take Dutch and go around back, just in case he tries to break out that way. Trish, you stay here with all these . . . good folks."

"What are you going to do?" she asked.

"I'm going in after him."

Susan had been standing just behind Robert D., and when she heard his last statement, she rushed up to him and put her hands on his shoulders.

"Robert D.," she said, "be careful. He has all kinds of guns in there, and he's probably just waiting for someone to come through that door."

"I know that," said Robert D.

"But you don't know where he is. After you get inside, you'll have to look for him."

"I know that, too. But on the other hand, he won't know which way I'm coming in. Don't worry, Susan. I'm not looking to get myself killed."

"There's one more thing," said Susan. "Don't forget about General."

Robert D. felt a chill run up his spine. It wasn't so much the thought of the beast as it was the sound of Susan's voice mentioning such a monster by a familiar name.

"Yeah," he said. "I know."

He started to turn away, but Susan pulled him to her and kissed his lips. Robert D. was a little embarrassed at this public display of emotion, but he took it like a man, then gently pushed her away. He pulled the borrowed revolver out of his waistband and checked it. It was a top-break Smith and Wesson .44, and it was fully loaded.

Inside the house, Brody had pulled his favorite chair around so that it faced the front door. It was in a direct line to the door and pushed back against the back wall of the living room. Brody sat in the chair with a double-barreled shotgun across his knees. A table beside the chair held a shotglass and a brandy bottle. On the other side of the chair, to Brody's left, General lay on the floor. When he realized that his small army of deputies was gone and he was alone, and when he saw the way in which the Drago residents had joined with Trish and Pawnee to march against him, Brody had realized that he was through. He had the money with which to hire more deputies, but he had waited too long. He had no way of locating suitable men. All his money was no good to him anymore. He considered surrendering and taking his chances with a trial. He might get off with a prison sentence. Could they pin any murders on him? He didn't think so. As far as he knew, no one had ever found McDowell.

Then the mob had gathered outside his house, and Brody knew that he could not surrender. There would be no trial. Those angry bastards would tear him to pieces. It was then that he realized he would die. It was all over. He would die, but he could control, to some extent, the manner of his death. He would not be torn to pieces by an angry mob, and he would not hang. They would have to come into the house after him, and he would be able to get one or two of them in the process. He hoped that he would get a chance to take Wade and that damned bitch girl, the sister of Bobby Madison. He poured himself a brandy and drank it, then refilled the glass. His left hand dropped casually down beside the chair and his fingers scratched the giant hound between the ears.

Chapter 23

The crowd grew silent as Robert D. climbed the stairs to the front porch of the blue house. He paused at the top of the stairs, then walked to the door. From inside, General set up a low, rolling, continuous bark. So the dog was in the front room. Robert D. stepped up to the front door and tried it. It was locked, as he had expected. He pounded on it with his fist and called out to Brody.

"Come on out," he said. Then he quickly stepped aside. A blast from a shotgun blew a hole in the door just about chest high. Robert D. stepped back to the porch rail, then changed directions again, and with two running steps, he leapt through a front window. He landed in a pile of glass and splinters on the living room floor and rolled. General was on him in a flash. Robert D. jammed the Smith and Wesson sideways between the great dripping jaws and pushed with all his strength to keep the fangs away from his face. Brody stood up and pointed the shotgun, but he hesitated. He did not want to kill the dog. General was his last ally, and there was still a mob outside. General was snarling and straining for Wade's throat. Robert D. had thrown a leg across the dog's body. The strength in his arms was slowly giving way. Brody still pointed the shotgun, undecided.

Outside Trish could not hold herself back. She had seen Robert D. throw himself through the window, and she could hear the sounds of his struggle with the snarling dog. Six-gun in hand, she ran up the steps to the broken window. Brody watched the movement through the window, and Trish saw the sheriff swing the gun around. She fell flat on the porch as the shotgun roared. Then she came back up to her knees and pushed her gun hand through the window, thumbing back the hammer at the same time. Brody threw the empty shotgun to one side and reached for a revolver, but Trish pulled the trigger before he could get his gun out of its holster. Her bullet struck him low in the abdomen. He jerked and hunkered forward, and he clutched at the pain with both his hands. Blood oozed out between his fingers and ran down his legs. Brody was harmless now but Robert D. was still in serious trouble, so Trish turned her gun on the beast. She couldn't get a clean shot from her angle at the window. She might hit Robert D. Trish climbed through the window, moved off to one side, and crouched for a low, sideways shot. She fired, and the fight was over. General slumped into death on top of Robert D. Robert D. lay still for a moment, catching his breath, then he shoved the dead animal to one side and got up, still panting and gasping for breath. Brody stood swaying, looking stunned. Trish looked at him, hatred in her eyes. She tried to remember Bobby, but it had been so long that she couldn't call up an image of his face. The only image that came into her mind was the one in the photograph on the granite spire in Phil Brody's backyard, the photograph taken of Bobby in death. She stretched out her arm to point her revolver at Brody's chest. Brody looked at her with stupid eyes. Trish thumbed back the hammer of her revolver. Robert D. took a step toward her.

"Trish?" he said.

She pulled the trigger and Brody fell over backward, dead.

They had to get some shovels from the hardware store and a wagon from the livery. They parked the wagon in the yard behind the blue house, but before they could do any digging, they had to remove all the granite rocks, the ones that Brody had piled on the grave to sell as souvenirs. When the rocks had all been tossed aside, Robert D., Pawnee, and Trish started digging. Claude and Dutch had offered to help, but Trish wouldn't have it.

"You've helped enough," she said. "This is family."

They took turns digging until they found and uncovered the coffin, a plain pine box, then lifted it out of the hole and loaded it onto the wagon. They tied the coffin securely to the wagonbed and fastened the tailgate in place. Then they loaded their personal belongings into the wagon and hitched a team of horses to it. They saddled their riding horses and were ready to go. Bobby would rest beside his parents in peaceful obscurity.

"One more thing," said Trish, taking the rope off her saddle. She threw a loop over the granite spire and pulled it over. Then she picked up one of the granite rocks and bashed the photograph to bits. Tossing the rock away, she looked at Robert D. and Pawnee.

"Now I'm ready," she said.

"I'll be right back," said Robert D. He walked up to the back door of the house and knocked. Susan opened the door and let him in.

"We're about ready to go," he said. "Are you packed?"

"Packed?" said Susan.

"Yeah. I thought you were going with me."

"I said I wanted to stay with you. I didn't mean that I wanted to leave Drago."

Robert D. was puzzled.

"There's too many bad memories here for you," he said. "You'd be better off to leave. Come with me."

"Robert D.," said Susan, slipping her arms over his shoulders, "I've got a home here. A nice one. I've got money in the bank. If you stay here with me, you could take Brody's place."

Robert D.'s face registered disgust, and he took hold of Susan's arms to extricate himself from her embrace.

"I didn't mean it like that," she said. "I meant that Drago is without a sheriff now. They'll take you. They'll want you. And even if they don't, you could take over. That's what Brody did, and you're more of a man than he was. You can get rich here, Robert D."

"Susan," said Robert D. "I thought you loved me, and I thought you'd go with me."

191

"Go where? To what? I need money and a nice home, Robert D. I can't live on love. Stay here with me. You've done your part for Trish. She doesn't need you anymore. She's got Pawnee to take care of her . . . as if she needed anyone to take care of her. Stay here."

"I killed too many people here, Susan," said Robert D. "I can't stay. And I ain't the kind of man you want."

He pulled himself free of her and headed for the back door.

"Robert D., you fool," said Susan. "Wait. Do you realize what you're throwing away here? Not just me. This whole town. It could all be yours."

Robert D. looked back at Susan.

"I don't want either one of you," he said. "God. You know, for a while there, I actually thought that . . . I loved you."

He walked out the door into the backyard and climbed onto his horse.

"Who's driving the wagon?" he asked.

"I will," said Trish.

"Good," said Robert D. "Let's take Bobby home."